CIRQUE DU FREAK

THE VAMPIRE'S ASSISTANT

My name is Darren Shan. I'm a half-vampire. I wasn't born that way. I lived at home with my parents and younger sister, Annie. I enjoyed school and had lots of friends. I liked reading horror stories and watching scary movies. When a freak show came to my town, my best friend got tickets, and we went. It was great, really spooky and weird. But the weirdest part came after the show.... Suddenly my days as a human were over. My nights as a vampire's assistant had begun.

Darren Shan is just an ordinary schoolboy until his visit to the Cirque Du Freak. Then Darren joins the powerful vampire Mr. Crepsley as his assistant, and they return to the mysterious freak show. There, Darren makes friends with the snake-boy, Evra Von. As he struggles with his new life as a vampire's assistant, Darren tries desperately to resist the temptation that sickens him...the one thing that can keep him alive. But destiny is calling.... The wolf-man is waiting....

CIRQUE DU FREAK

THE VAMPIRE'S ASSISTANT

{BOOK 2}

by
DARREN SHAN

LITTLE, BROWN AND COMPANY

New York   Boston

Little, Brown and Company

Hachette Book Group
237 Park Avenue, New York, NY 10017
Visit our Web site at www.lb-teens.com

Little, Brown and Company is a division of Hachette Book Group, Inc.
The Little, Brown name and logo are trademarks of Hachette Book Group, Inc.

First U.S. Hardcover Edition: April 2001
First U.S. Paperback Edition: June 2002
First published in Great Britain by Collins in 2000.

Library of Congress Cataloging-in-Publication Data

Shan, Darren.
    The vampire's assistant — 1st U.S. ed.
    p. cm. (The saga of Darren Shan ; bk.2)
    Sequel to Cirque Du Freak.
    Summary: After traveling with Mr. Crepsley, the vampire who
made him into a half-vampire, Darren returns to the freak show
known as the Cirque Du Freak and continues to fight his need to
drink human blood.
    ISBN 978-0-316-60610-3 (hc) / 978-0-316-60684-4 (pb)
    [1. Vampires — Fiction. 2. Spiders — Fiction. 3. Best
friends — Fiction. 2. Freak shows — Fiction.] I. Title.
PZ7.S5283 Vam 2001
[Fic] — dc21   2001016518

HC: 10 9 8 7 6 5 4 3 2 1
PB: 10

RRD-C

Printed in the United States of America

For:

Granny and Grandad—tough old fogeys

OBEs (Order of the Bloody Entrails) to:
Caroline "Tracker" Paul
Paul "The Pillager" Litherland

Heads off to:
Biddy "Jekyll" and Liam "Hyde"
Gillie "Grave Robber" Russell
The hideously creepy HarperCollins gang
and
Emma and Chris (from "Ghouls Are Us")

INTRODUCTION

MY NAME IS Darren Shan. I'm a half-vampire.

I wasn't born that way. I used to be ordinary. I lived at home with my parents and younger sister, Annie. I enjoyed school and had lots of friends.

I liked reading horror stories and watching scary movies. When this freak show came to town, my best friend, Steve Leopard, got tickets, and we went together. It was great, really spooky and weird. A super night out.

But the weirdest part came after the show. Steve recognized one of the characters from the show. He'd seen a drawing of him in an old book and knew he was — a *vampire*. Steve stuck around after the show and asked the vampire to turn *him* into one, too! Mr. Crepsley — the vampire — would have, but he found out Steve's blood was evil, and that was the end of that.

Or it *would* have been the end, except *I* stuck around, too, to see what Steve was up to.

I wanted nothing to do with vampires, but I'd always loved spiders — I used to keep them as pets — and Mr. Crepsley had a poisonous performing tarantula, Madam Octa, who could do all sorts of great tricks. I stole her and left a note for the vampire, saying I'd tell people about him if he came after me.

To make a long story short, Madam Octa bit Steve and he ended up in the hospital. He would have died, so I went to Mr. Crepsley and asked him to save Steve. He agreed, but in return *I had to become a half-vampire and travel with him as his assistant!*

I ran away after he'd turned me into a half-vampire (by pumping part of his own horrible blood into me) and saved Steve. But then I realized I was hungry for blood, and was afraid I'd do something terrible (like bite my sister) if I stayed at home.

So Mr. Crepsley helped me fake my death. I was buried alive, and then, in the dead of night, with no one around, he dug me up and we took off together. My days as a human were over. My nights as a vampire's assistant had begun.

CHAPTER ONE

IT WAS A DRY, WARM NIGHT, and Stanley Collins had decided to walk home after the Boy Scouts meeting. It wasn't a very long walk — less than a mile — and though the night was dark, he knew every step of the way as surely as he knew how to tie a reef knot.

Stanley was a scoutmaster. He loved the Scouts. He'd been one when he was a boy and kept in contact when he grew up. He'd turned his own three sons into first-rate Scouts, and now that they'd grown up and left home, he was helping the local kids.

Stanley walked quickly to keep warm. He was only wearing shorts and a T-shirt, and even though it was a nice night, his arms and legs were soon covered in goosebumps. He didn't mind. His wife would have a delicious cup of hot chocolate and cookies waiting for him when he got home. He'd enjoy them all the more after a good, brisk walk.

Trees grew along both sides of the road home, making it very dark and dangerous for anyone who wasn't used to it. But Stanley had no fears. On the contrary, he loved the night. He enjoyed listening to the sound of his feet crunching through the grass and briars.

Crunch. Crunch. Crunch.

He smiled. When his sons were young, he'd often pretended there were monsters lying in wait up in the trees as they walked home. He'd make scary noises and shake the leaves of low-hanging branches when the boys weren't looking. Sometimes they'd burst into screams and run for home at top speed, and Stanley would follow after them, laughing.

Crunch. Crunch. Crunch.

Sometimes, if he was having trouble getting to sleep at night, he would imagine the sounds of his feet as they made their way home, and that always helped him drift off into a happy dream.

Crunch. Crunch. Crunch.

It was the nicest sound in the world, as far as Stanley was concerned. It was a great feeling, to know you were all alone and safe as can be.

Crunch. Crunch. Crunch.

Snap.

Stanley stopped and frowned. That had sounded like a stick breaking — but how could it have been? He would have felt it if he'd stepped on a twig. And there were no cows or sheep in the nearby fields.

He stood still for about half a minute, listening curiously. When there were no more sounds, he shook his head and smiled. It had been his imagination playing tricks on him, that was all. He'd tell the wife about it when he got home and they'd have a good old laugh.

He started walking again.

Crunch. Crunch. Crunch.

There. Back to the familiar sounds. There was nobody else around. He would have heard more than a single branch snapping if there was. Nobody could creep up on Stanley J. Collins. He was a trained scoutmaster. His ears were as sharp as a fox's.

Crunch. Crunch. Crunch. Crunch. Cru —

Snap.

Stanley stopped again and, for the first time, the fingers of fear began to squeeze around his beating heart.

That hadn't been his imagination. He'd heard it, clear as a bell. A twig snapping, somewhere overhead. And before it snapped — had there been the slightest rustling sound, like something moving?

Stanley gazed up at the trees but it was too dark to see. There could have been a monster the size of a car up there and he wouldn't have been able to spot it. Ten monsters! A hundred! A thou—

Oh, that was silly. There were no monsters in the trees. Monsters didn't exist. Everyone knew that. Monsters weren't real. It was a squirrel or an owl up there, something ordinary like that.

Stanley raised a foot and began to bring it down.

Snap.

His foot hung in the air, midstep, and his heart pounded quickly. That was no squirrel! The sound was too sharp. Something *big* was up there. Something that shouldn't be up there. Something that had never been up there before. Something that —

Snap!

The sound was closer this time, lower down, and suddenly Stanley could stand it no longer.

He began to run.

Stanley was a large man, but pretty fit for his age. Still, it had been a long time since he'd run this fast, and after a hundred yards he was out of breath and had a cramp in his side.

He slowed to a halt and bent over, gasping for air.

Crunch.

His head shot up.

CHAPTER FOUR

BLOOD . . .

Mr. Crepsley spent a lot of his time teaching me about blood. It's vital to vampires. Without it we grow weak and old and die. Blood keeps us young. Vampires age at a tenth the human rate (for every ten years that pass vampires only age one), but without human blood, we age even quicker than humans, maybe twenty or thirty years within a year or two. As a half-vampire, who aged at a fifth the human rate, I didn't have to drink as much human blood as Mr. Crepsley — but I would have to drink some to live.

The blood of animals — dogs, cows, sheep — keeps vampires going, but there are some animals they — *we* — can't drink from: cats, for instance. If a vampire drinks a cat's blood, he might as well pour poison down his throat. We also can't drink from monkeys, frogs, most fish, or snakes.

Mr. Crepsley hadn't told me the names of all the dangerous animals. There were a whole lot, and it would take time to learn them all. His advice was to always ask before I tried something new.

Vampires have to feed on humans about once a month. Most feast once a week. That way, they don't have to suck much blood. If you only feed once a month, you have to drink a lot of blood at one time.

Mr. Crepsley said it was dangerous to go too long without drinking. He said the thirst could make you drink more than you meant to, and then you were probably going to end up killing the person you drank from.

"A vampire who feasts frequently can control himself," he said. "One who drinks only when he must will end up sucking wildly. The hunger inside us must be fed to be controlled."

Fresh blood was the best. If you drink from a living human, the blood is full of goodness and you don't need to take very much. But blood begins to go sour when a person dies. If you drink from a dead body, you have to drink a lot more.

"The general rule is, never drink from a person

who has been dead more than a day," Mr. Crepsley explained.

"How will I know how long a person's been dead?" I asked.

"The taste of the blood," he said. "You will learn to tell good blood from bad. Bad blood is like sour milk, only worse."

"Is drinking bad blood dangerous?" I asked.

"Yes. It will sicken you, maybe turn you crazy or even kill you."

Brrrr!

We could bottle fresh blood and keep it for as long as we liked, for use in emergencies. Mr. Crepsley had a few bottles of blood stored in his cloak. He sometimes had one with a meal, as if it were a small bottle of wine.

"Could you survive on bottled blood alone?" I asked one night.

"For a while," he said. "But not in the long run."

"How do you bottle it?" I asked, examining one of the glass bottles. It was like a test tube, only the glass was darker and thicker.

"It is tricky," he said. "I will show you how it is done, the next time I am filling up."

Blood . . .

It was what I needed most, but also what I feared most. If I drank a human's blood, there was no going back. I'd be a vampire for life. If I avoided it, I might become a human again. Maybe the vampire blood in my veins would wear out. Maybe I wouldn't die. Maybe only the vampire in me would die, and then I could go home to my family and friends.

It wasn't much of a hope — Mr. Crepsley had said it was impossible to become human again — but it was the only dream I had to hold on to.

CHAPTER FIVE

DAYS AND NIGHTS PASSED, and we moved on. We wandered from towns to villages to cities. I wasn't getting along very well with Mr. Crepsley. Nice as he was, I couldn't forget that he was the one who'd pumped vampire blood into my veins and made it impossible for me to stay with my family.

I hated him. Sometimes, during the day, I'd think about driving a stake through his heart while he was sleeping, and running away. I might have, too, except I knew I couldn't survive without him. For the moment I needed Larten Crepsley. But when the day came that I could look after myself . . .

I was in charge of Madam Octa. I had to find food for her and exercise her and clean out her cage. I didn't want to — I hated the spider almost as much as I hated the vampire — but Mr. Crepsley said I was the one who'd stolen her, so I had to look after her.

I practiced a few tricks with her every now and then, but my heart wasn't in it. She didn't interest me anymore, and as the weeks went by I played with her less and less.

The one good thing about being on the road was being able to visit a whole bunch of places I hadn't been before and see a lot of cool sights. I loved traveling. But, since we traveled at night, I didn't get to see many of our surroundings — bummer!

One day, while Mr. Crepsley was sleeping, I got tired of being indoors. I left a note on the TV, in case I wasn't back when he woke up, then left. I only had a little money and had no idea where I would go, but that didn't matter. Just getting out of the hotel and spending some time by myself was wonderful.

It was a large town but pretty quiet. I checked out a few arcades and played some video games in them. I'd never been very good at video games before, but with my new reflexes and skills I was able to do pretty much anything I wanted.

I raced through all levels, knocked out every opponent in martial arts tournaments, and zapped all the aliens attacking from the skies in the sci-fi adventures.

After that I toured the town. There were plenty of

fountains and statues and parks and museums, all of which I checked out with interest. But going around the museums reminded me of Mom — she loved taking me to museums — and that upset me: I always felt lonely and miserable when I thought of Mom, Dad, or Annie.

I spotted a group of guys my age playing hockey on a cement playground. There were eight players on each side. Most had plastic sticks, though a few had wooden ones. They were using an old tennis ball as a puck.

I stopped to watch, and after a few minutes one of the guys came over to me.

"Where are you from?" he asked.

"Out of town," I said. "I'm staying at a hotel with my father." I hated calling Mr. Crepsley that, but it was the safest thing to say.

"He's from out of town," the boy called back to the other guys, who had stopped playing.

"Is he part of the Addams Family?" one of them shouted back, and they all laughed.

"What's that supposed to mean?" I asked, offended.

"Have you looked at yourself in a mirror lately?" the boy said.

I glanced down at my dusty suit and knew why

they were laughing: I looked like something out of *Beetlejuice*.

"I lost the bag with my normal clothes," I lied. "These are all I have. I'm getting new stuff soon."

"You should." The boy smiled, then asked if I played hockey. When I said yes, he invited me to play with them.

"You can be on my team," he said, handing me a spare stick. "We're down, six–two. My name's Michael."

"Hey. I'm Darren," I replied, testing the stick.

I rolled up the cuffs of my pants and made sure my shoelaces were double-tied. While I was doing that, the other team scored another goal. Michael swore loudly and dragged the ball back to the center.

"You ready to go?" he asked me.

"Sure."

"Come on, then," he said. He tapped the ball to me and moved ahead, waiting for me to pass back.

It had been a long time since I'd played hockey — at school, in gym, we'd usually had to choose between hockey and soccer, and I never passed up a chance for a game of soccer — but with the stick in my hands and the ball at my feet, it seemed like only yesterday since I'd played hockey.

I knocked the ball from left to right a few times, making sure I hadn't forgotten how to control it, then looked up and focused on the goal.

There were seven players between me and the goalie. None of them rushed to stop me. I guess they felt they didn't need to since they were five goals ahead.

I started running. A big kid — the other team's captain — tried blocking me, but I slipped around him easily. I was past another two before they could react, then dribbled around a fourth. The fifth player slid in with his stick at knee level, but I jumped over him with ease, faked the sixth, and shot before the seventh and final defender could get in the way.

Even though I hit the ball pretty softly, it went a lot harder than the goalie was expecting and flew into the top right-hand corner of the goal. It bounced off the wall and I caught it in the air.

I turned, smiling, and looked back at my teammates. They were still back near the other goal, staring at me in shock. I carried the ball back to the center line and set it down without saying a word. Then I turned to Michael and said, "Seven–three."

He blinked slowly, then smiled. "Oh, yeah!" he cheered softly, then high-fived his teammates. "I think we're going to enjoy this!"

I had a great time for a while, dominating play, rushing back to defend, picking players out with pin-point passes. I scored a couple of goals and set up four more. We were leading 9–7 and coasting. The other team hated it. They made us give them two of our best players, but it made no difference. I could have given them everybody except our goalie and still kicked their butts.

Then things got nasty. The captain of the other team — Danny — had been trying to foul me for a while, but I was too quick for him and easily dodged his raised stick and stuck-out legs. But then he began to punch my ribs and stand on my toes and slam his el-bows into my arms. None of it hurt me, but it annoyed me. I hate sore losers.

The last straw came when Danny pinched me in a *very* painful place! Even vampires have their limits. I yelled out and bent over, wincing from the pain.

Danny laughed and took off with the ball.

I got up after a few seconds, mad as hell. Danny was halfway down the rink. I sprinted after him. I knocked the players between us aside — it didn't mat-ter if they were on his team or mine — then caught up behind him and swiped at his legs with my stick. It would have been a dangerous tackle if it had come from a human. Coming from a half-vampire . . .

There was a sharp snapping sound. Danny screamed and went down. Play stopped immediately. Everybody in the game knew the difference between a yell of pain and a scream of real agony.

I scrambled to my feet, already sorry for what I'd done, wishing I could take it back. I looked at my stick, hoping to find it broken in two, hoping that had been what made the snapping noise. But it wasn't.

I'd broken both of Danny's shinbones.

His lower legs were bent awkwardly and the skin around the shins was torn. I could see the white of bone in among the red.

Michael bent over to examine Danny's legs. When he got up, there was a horrified look in his eyes.

"You've cracked his legs wide open!" he gasped.

"I didn't mean to," I cried. "He squeezed my . . ." I pointed to the spot beneath my waist.

"You broke his legs!" Michael shouted, then backed away from me. Everyone around him backed away as well.

They were *afraid* of me.

Breathing hard, I dropped my stick and left, knowing I'd make matters worse if I stayed and waited for grown-ups to arrive. None of the guys tried to stop me. They were too scared. They were terrified of me . . . Darren Shan . . . a *monster.*

CHAPTER SIX

IT WAS DARK when I got back. Mr. Crepsley was awake. I told him we should leave town right away, but didn't tell him why. He took one look at my face, nodded, and started gathering our stuff.

We didn't say much that night. I was thinking how much it stunk to be a half-vampire. Mr. Crepsley could tell there was something wrong with me, but didn't bother me with questions. It wasn't the first time I'd been grouchy. He was getting used to my mood swings.

We found an abandoned church to sleep in. Mr. Crepsley lay out on a long pew, while I made a bed for myself on a pile of moss and weeds on the floor.

I woke early and spent the day exploring the church and the small cemetery outside. The headstones were old and a lot of them were cracked or covered with weeds. I spent a few hours cleaning some, pulling weeds away and washing the stones with water I got from a nearby stream. It kept my mind off the hockey game.

A family of rabbits lived in a nearby burrow. As the day went by, they crept closer to see what I was up to. They were curious little guys, especially the young ones. At one point, I pretended to be asleep and a couple edged closer and closer, until they were only a few feet away.

When they were as close as they would probably come, I leaped up and shouted, "Boo!" and they went running away like wildfire. One fell head over heels and rolled away down the mouth of the burrow.

That totally cheered me up.

I found a grocery store in the afternoon and bought some meat and vegetables. I made a fire when I got back to the church, then grabbed the pots and pans bag from underneath Mr. Crepsley's pew. I looked through the contents until I found what I was looking for. It was a small pot. I carefully laid it upside down on the floor, then pressed the metal bulge on the top.

The pot mushroomed out in size, as folded-in panels opened up. Within five seconds it had become a full-sized pot, which I filled with water and stuck on the fire.

All the pots and pans in the bag were like this. Mr.

Crepsley got them from a woman called Evanna a long time ago. They weighed the same as ordinary cookware, but because they could fold up small, they were easier to carry around.

I made a stew like Mr. Crepsley had taught me. He thought everybody should know how to cook.

I took leftover pieces of the carrots and cabbage outside and dropped them by the rabbit burrow.

Mr. Crepsley was surprised to find dinner — which was breakfast from his point of view — waiting for him when he awoke. He sniffed the fumes from the bubbling pot and licked his lips.

"I could get used to this." He smiled, then yawned, stretched, and ran a hand through the short crop of orange hair on his head. Then he scratched the long scar running down the left side of his face. It was a familiar routine of his.

I'd always wanted to ask how he got his scar, but I never had. One night, when I was feeling brave, I would.

There were no tables, so we ate off our laps. I got two of the folded-up plates out of the bag, popped them open, and grabbed knives and forks. I served the food and we ate.

Toward the end, Mr. Crepsley wiped around his mouth with a white napkin and coughed awkwardly.

"The stew is very nice," he complimented me.

"Thank you," I replied.

"I . . . um . . . that is . . ." He sighed. "I never was very good at being subtle," he said, "so I will come right out and say it: What went wrong yesterday? Why were you so upset?"

I stared at my almost empty plate, not sure if I wanted to answer or not. Then, all of a sudden, I blurted out the whole story. I hardly took a breath between the start and the finish.

Mr. Crepsley listened carefully. When I was done, he thought about it for a minute or two before speaking.

"It is something you must get used to," he said. "It is a fact of life that we are stronger than humans, faster and tougher. If you play with them, they will be hurt."

"I didn't mean to hurt him," I said. "It was an accident."

Mr. Crepsley shrugged. "Listen, Darren, there is no way you can stop this from happening again, not if you interact with humans. No matter how hard you try to be normal, you are not. There will always be accidents waiting to happen."

"What you're saying is, I can't have friends anymore, right?" I nodded sadly. "I'd figured that out by myself. That's why I was so sad. I was getting used to the idea of never being able to go back home to see my old friends, but it was just yesterday that I realized I'd never be able to make new ones, either. I'm stuck with *you*. I can't have any other friends, can I?"

He rubbed his scar and pursed his lips. "That is not true," he said. "You can have friends. You just have to be careful. You —"

"That's not good enough!" I cried. "You said it yourself; there will always be an accident waiting to happen. Even shaking hands is dangerous. I could cut their wrists open with my nails!"

I shook my head slowly. "No," I said firmly. "I won't put people's lives in danger. I'm too dangerous to have friends anymore. Besides, it's not like I can make a true friend."

"Why not?" he asked.

"True friends don't keep secrets from one another. I could never tell a human that I was a vampire. I'd always have to lie and pretend to be someone I'm not. I'd always be afraid he'd find out what I was and hate me."

"It is a problem every vampire shares," Mr. Crepsley said.

"But every vampire isn't a child!" I shouted. "What age were you when you were changed? Were you a man?" He nodded. "Friends aren't that important to adults. My dad told me that grown-ups get used to not having a lot of friends. They have work and hobbies and other stuff to keep them busy. But my friends were the most important thing in my life, besides my family. Well, you took my family away when you pumped your stinking blood into me. Now you've ruined the chances of my ever having a real friend again.

"Thanks a lot," I said angrily. "Thanks for making a monster out of me and wrecking my life."

I was close to tears, but didn't want to cry, not in front of him. So I stabbed the last piece of meat on my plate with my fork and rammed it into my mouth, then I chewed on it fiercely.

Mr. Crepsley was quiet after my outburst. I couldn't tell if he was angry or sorry. For a while I thought I'd said too much. What if he turned around and said, "If that's the way you feel, I will leave you"? What would I do then?

I was thinking of apologizing when he spoke in a soft voice and surprised me.

"I am sorry," he said. "I should not have blooded you. It was a poor call. You were too young. It has been so long since I was a boy, I had forgotten what it was like. I never thought of your friends and how much you would miss them. It was wrong of me to blood you. Terribly wrong. I . . ."

He trailed off into silence. He looked so miserable, I almost felt sorry for him. Then I remembered what he'd done to me and I hated him again. Then I saw wet drops at the corners of his eyes that might have been tears, and I felt sorry for him again.

I was really confused.

"Well, there's no use crying about it," I finally said. "We can't go back. What's done is done, right?"

"Yes." He sighed. "If I could, I would take back my terrible gift. But that is not possible. Vampirism is forever. Once somebody has been changed, there is no changing back.

"Still," he said, mulling it over, "it is not as bad as you think. Perhaps . . ." His eyes narrowed thoughtfully.

"Perhaps what?" I asked.

"We *can* find friends for you," he said. "You do not have to be stuck with me all the time."

"I don't understand." I frowned. "Didn't we just agree it wasn't safe for me to be around humans?"

"I am not talking about humans," he said, starting to smile. "I am talking about people with special powers. People like us. People you can tell your secrets to. . . ."

He leaned across and took my hands in his.

"Darren," he said, "what do you think about going back and becoming a member of the Cirque Du Freak?"

CHAPTER SEVEN

THE MORE WE DISCUSSED the idea, the more I liked it.
Mr. Crepsley said the Cirque performers would know
what I was and would accept me as one of their own.
The lineup of the show changed a lot and there was almost always someone who would be around my own
age. I could hang out with them.

"What if I don't like it there?" I asked.

"Then we leave," he said. "I enjoyed traveling with
the Cirque, but I am not crazy about it. If you like it,
we stay. If you do not, we hit the road again."

"They won't mind me tagging along?" I asked.

"You will have to pull your weight," he replied.
"Mr. Tall insists on everybody doing something. You
will have to help set up chairs and lights, sell souvenirs, clean up afterward, or do the cooking. You will

be kept busy, but they will not overwork you. We will have plenty of time for our lessons."

We decided to give it a shot. At least it would mean a real bed every night. My back was stiff from sleeping on floors.

Mr. Crepsley had to find out where the show was before we could join. I asked him how he was going to do that. He told me he was able to home in on Mr. Tall's thoughts.

"You mean he's telepathic?" I asked, remembering what Steve had called people who could talk to each other using only their brains.

"Sort of," Mr. Crepsley said. "We cannot speak to each other with our thoughts but I can pick up his . . . *aura*, you could call it. Once I locate that, tracking him down will be no problem."

"Could I locate his aura?" I wanted to know.

"No," Mr. Crepsley said. "Most vampires — along with a few gifted humans — can, but half-vampires cannot."

He sat down in the middle of the church and closed his eyes. He was quiet for about a minute. Then his eyelids opened and he stood.

"Got him," he said.

"So soon?" I asked. "I thought it would take longer."

"I have searched for his aura many times," Mr.

"Here?" I piped up in surprise.

"That puzzles you?" Mr. Tall enquired.

"It's in the middle of nowhere," I said. "I thought you only played in towns and cities, where you'd get big audiences."

"We *always* get a big audience," Mr. Tall said. "No matter where we play, people will come. Usually we stick to more populated areas, but this is a slow time of the year for us. As I've said, several of our best performers are absent, as are . . . certain other members of our company."

A strange, secretive look passed between Mr. Tall and Mr. Crepsley, and I felt I was being left out of something.

"So we are resting for a while," Mr. Tall went on. "We shall not be putting on any shows for a few days. We're relaxing."

"We passed a camp on our way," Mr. Crepsley said. "Are they causing any problems?"

"The foot soldiers of NOP?" Mr. Tall laughed. "They're too busy defending trees and rocks to interfere with us."

"What's NOP?" I asked.

"Nature's Opposing Protectors," Mr. Tall explained. "They're ecowarriors. They run around the country trying to stop new roads and bridges from being built. They've been here a couple of months but are due to move on soon."

"Are they real warriors?" I asked. "Do they have guns and grenades and tanks?"

The two adults almost laughed their heads off.

"He can be quite silly sometimes," Mr. Crepsley said between fits of laughter, "but he is not as dumb as he seems."

I felt my face reddening but held my tongue. I knew from experience that it was no use getting mad at grown-ups when they laugh at you; it only makes them laugh even harder.

"They call themselves warriors," Mr. Tall said, "but they're not really. They chain themselves to trees and pour sand into the engines of backhoes and toss nails in the paths of cars. That sort of thing."

"Why —," I started, but Mr. Crepsley interrupted.

"We do not have time for questions," he said. "A few more minutes and the sun will be up." He rose and shook Mr. Tall's hand. "Thank you for taking us back, Hibernius."

"My pleasure," Mr. Tall replied.

"I trust you took good care of my coffin?"

"Of course."

Mr. Crepsley smiled happily and rubbed his hands

together. "That is what I miss most when I am away. It will be nice to sleep in it once more."

"What about the boy?" Mr. Tall asked. "Do you want us to knock together a coffin for him?"

"Don't even think about it!" I shouted. "You won't get me in one of those again!" I remembered what it felt like to be in a coffin — when I was buried alive — and shivered.

Mr. Crepsley smiled. "Put Darren in with one of the other performers," he said. "Somebody his own age, if possible."

Mr. Tall thought a moment. "How about Evra?"

Mr. Crepsley's smile spread. "Yes. I think putting him in with Evra is a marvelous idea."

"Who's Evra?" I asked nervously.

"You will find out," Mr. Crepsley promised, opening the door to the van. "I will leave you to Mr. Tall. He will take care of you. I have to be away."

And then he was gone, off to find his beloved coffin.

I glanced over my shoulder and saw Mr. Tall standing directly behind me. I don't know how he crossed the room so quickly. I didn't even hear him moving to stand up.

"Shall we go?" he said.

I gulped and nodded.

He led the way through the campsite. The morning was breaking and I saw a couple of lights coming on in a few of the vans and tents. Mr. Tall led me to an old gray tent, big enough for five or six people.

"Here are some blankets," he said, handing over a bunch of woolly sheets. "And a pillow." I didn't know where he got them from — he didn't have them when we left the van — but was too tired to ask. "You may sleep as late as you wish. I will come for you when you are awake and explain your duties. Evra will take care of you until then."

I lifted the flap of the tent and looked inside. It was too dark to see anything. "Who's Evra?" I asked, turning back to Mr. Tall. But he was gone, having disappeared with his usual quick, silent speed.

I sighed and entered, clutching the blankets to my chest. I let the flap fall back into place, then stood quietly inside, waiting for my eyes to adjust. I could hear someone breathing softly and could make out a vague shape in a hammock in the darkness beyond the middle of the tent. I looked for somewhere to make my bed. I didn't want my tentmate tripping over me when he was getting up.

I walked forward a few blind steps. Suddenly something slithered toward me through the darkness.

I stopped and stared ahead, wishing so badly that I could see (without the light of the stars or moon, even a vampire struggles to make things out).

"Hello?" I whispered. "Are you Evra? I'm Darren Shan. I'm your new —"

I stopped. The slithering noise had reached my feet. As I stood rooted to the spot, something fleshy and slimy wrapped itself around my legs. I instantly knew what it was but didn't dare look down until it had climbed more than halfway up my body. Finally, as its coils curled around my chest, I worked up the courage to look down and stare into the eyes of a long, thick, hissing . . . snake!

CHAPTER EIGHT

I STOOD FROZEN with fear for more than an hour, staring into the snake's deathly cold eyes, waiting for it to strike.

Finally, with the light of the strong morning sun shining through the canvas of the tent, the sleeping shape in the hammock shifted, yawned, sat up, and glanced around.

It was the snake-boy, and he looked shocked when he saw me. He immediately rocked back in the hammock and raised the covers, as though to protect himself. Then he saw the snake wrapped around me and breathed easily.

"Who are you?" he asked sharply. "What are you doing here?"

I shook my head slowly. I didn't dare speak for fear

that the movement of my lungs would cause the snake to strike.

"You'd better answer," he warned, "or I'll tell her to take your eyes out."

"I . . . I . . . I'm Duh-Darren Sh-sh-Shan," I stuttered. "Mr. Tuh-Tall told me to cuh-come in. He said I wuh-wuh-was supposed to be your new ruh-ruh-ruh-roommate."

"Darren Shan?" The snake-boy frowned, then pointed knowingly. "You're Mr. Crepsley's assistant, aren't you?"

"Yes," I said quietly.

The snake-boy grinned. "Did he know Mr. Tall was putting you in with me?" I nodded and he laughed. "I've never met a vampire without a nasty sense of humor."

He swung down out of the hammock, crossed the tent, took hold of the snake's head, and began unwrapping it. "You're okay," he assured me. "In fact, you were never in danger. The snake's been asleep the whole time. You could have tugged her off and she wouldn't have stirred. She's a deep sleeper."

"She's *asleep?*" I squeaked. "But . . . how come she wrapped herself around me?"

He smiled. "She sleepcrawls."

"Sleepcrawls!" I stared at him, then at the snake, which hadn't moved while he was unwinding her. The last of her coils came free and I could step away to one side. My legs were stiff and full of pins and needles.

"A sleepcrawling snake." I laughed uneasily. "Thank God she's not a sleep*eating* snake!"

The snake-boy tucked his pet away in a corner and stroked her head lovingly. "She wouldn't have eaten you even if she had woken up," he informed me. "She ate a goat yesterday. Snakes her size don't have to eat very often."

Leaving his snake, he threw back the tent flap and stepped out. I followed quickly, not wanting to be left alone with the reptile.

I studied him closely outside. He was exactly as I remembered: a few years older than me and very thin, with long yellow-green hair, narrow eyes, and strangely webbed fingers and toes; his body was covered in green, gold, yellow, and blue scales. He was wearing a pair of shorts and nothing else.

"By the way," he said, "my name's Evra Von." He held out a hand and we shook. His palm felt slippery, but dry. A few of the scales came off and stuck to my hand when I pulled it away. They were like scraps of colored dead skin.

"Evra Von what?" I asked.

"Just plain Von," he said, rubbing his stomach. "You hungry?"

"Yes," I said, and went with Evra to get something to eat.

The camp was alive with activity. Since there had been no show the night before, most of the freaks and their helpers had gone to bed early, and so now they were up and about earlier than usual.

I was fascinated by the hustle and bustle. I hadn't realized there were so many people working for the Cirque. I'd thought it would just be the performers and assistants I'd seen the night I went to the show with Steve, but as I looked around I saw that those were just the tip of the iceberg. There were at least two dozen people walking or talking, washing or cooking, none of whom I'd seen before.

"Who are all these?" I asked.

"The backbone of the Cirque Du Freak," Evra replied. "They do the driving, set up the tents, do the laundry and the cooking, fix our costumes, clean up after shows. It's a big operation."

"Are they normal humans?" I asked.

"Most of them," he said.

"How did they come to work here?"

"Some are related to the performers. Some are

friends of Mr. Tall. Some just wandered in, liked what they saw, and stayed."

"People can do that?" I asked.

"If Mr. Tall likes the look of them," Evra said. "There are always openings at the Cirque Du Freak."

Evra stopped at a large campfire, and I stopped beside him. Hans Hands (a man who could walk on his hands and run faster on them than the world's fastest sprinter) was resting on a log, while Truska (the bearded lady, who grew her beard whenever she wanted) cooked sausages on a wooden stick. Several humans were sitting or lying around.

"Good morning, Evra Von," Hans Hands said.

"How are you, Hans?" Evra replied.

"Who's your young friend?" Hans asked, eyeing me suspiciously.

"This is Darren Shan," Evra said.

"*The* Darren Shan?" Hans asked, eyebrows raising.

"None other." Evra grinned.

"What do you mean, '*The* Darren Shan'?" I asked.

"You're famous in these parts," Hans said.

"Why? Because I'm a" — I lowered my voice — "half-vampire?"

Hans laughed pleasantly. "Half-vampires are nothing new. If I had a silver dollar for every half-vampire

I'd seen, I'd have . . ." He scrunched up his face and thought. "Twenty-nine silver dollars. But *young* half-vampires are a different story. I never saw or heard of a guy your age living it up among the ranks of the walking dead. Tell me: Have the Vampire Generals been around to inspect you yet?"

"Who are the Vampire Generals?" I asked.

"They're —"

"Hans!" a lady washing clothes barked. He stopped speaking and looked around guiltily. "Do you think Larten would enjoy hearing you spreading tales?" she snapped.

Hans made a face. "Sorry," he said. "It's the morning air. I'm not used to it. It makes me say things I shouldn't."

I wanted him to explain about the Vampire Generals, but I guess it would have been impolite to ask.

Truska checked the sausages, pulled a couple off the stick, and handed them out. She smiled when she came to me, and said something in a strange, foreign language.

Evra laughed. "She wants to know if you like sausages or if you're a vegetarian."

"That's a good one!" Hans chuckled. "A vampire vegetarian!"

"You speak her language?" I asked Evra.

"Yes," he said proudly. "I'm still learning — it's the hardest language I've ever tried to learn — but I'm the only one in the camp who knows what she's saying. I'm excellent at languages," he bragged.

"What language is it?" I asked.

"I don't know," he said, frowning. "She won't tell me."

That sounded weird, but I didn't want to say anything to offend him. Instead, I took one of the sausages and smiled thanks. I bit into it and had to drop it immediately; it was piping hot! Evra laughed and handed me a glass of water. I drank until my mouth was back to normal, then blew on the sausage to cool it down.

We sat with Hans and Truska and the others for a while, chatting and eating and soaking up the morning sun. The grass was wet with dew, but none of us minded. Evra introduced me to everyone in the group. There were too many names for me to remember at once, so I just smiled and shook hands.

Mr. Tall soon appeared. One minute he wasn't there, the next he was standing behind Evra, warming his hands over the fire.

"You're up early, Master Shan," Mr. Tall remarked.

"I couldn't sleep," I told him. "I was too —" I looked over at Evra and smiled "— wound-up."

"I hope it will not affect your ability to work," Mr. Tall said.

"I'll be fine," I said. "I'm ready to work."

"You're sure?"

"I'm sure."

"That's what I like to hear." He pulled out a large notebook and flipped through the pages. "Let's see what we can find for you to do today," he said. "Tell me: Are you a good cook?"

"I can cook stew. Mr. Crepsley taught me."

"Have you ever cooked for thirty or forty humans?"

"No."

"Too bad. Maybe you'll learn." He flipped through another couple of pages. "Can you sew?"

"No."

"Have you washed clothes before?"

"By hand?"

"Yes."

"No."

"Hmmm." He flipped some more, then snapped the book shut. "Okay," he said, "until we find a more permanent position for you, stick with Evra and help him with his chores. Does that sound fair?"

"I'd like that," I said.

"You don't mind, Evra?" he asked the snake-boy.

"Not at all," Evra replied.

"Very well. It's settled. Evra will be in charge of you until further notice. Do what he says. When your colleague-in-blood arises" — he meant Mr. Crepsley — "you're free to spend the night with him if he so desires. We'll see how you do, then make a decision on how best to utilize your talents."

"Thank you," I said.

"My pleasure," he replied.

I expected him to suddenly vanish then, but instead he turned and walked away slowly, whistling, enjoying the sunshine.

"Well, Darren," Evra said, sticking a scaly arm around my shoulders, "looks like you and I are partners now. How do you feel about that?"

"I feel good . . . partner."

"Cool!" He slapped my shoulder and gulped down the last of his sausage. "Then let's get going."

"What do we do first?" I asked.

"What we'll be doing first every morning," Evra said. "Milking the poison from the fangs of my snake."

"Oh," I said. "Is it dangerous?"

"Only if she bites before we finish," Evra said, then laughed at my expression and pushed me ahead of him to the tent.

CHAPTER NINE

Evra did the milking himself — to my great relief — then we brought the snake outside and laid her on the grass. We grabbed buckets of water and scrubbed her down with really soft sponges.

After that, we had to feed the wolf-man. His cage was near the back of the campsite. He roared when he saw us coming. He looked as angry and dangerous as he had that night I went to see the Cirque with Steve. He shook the bars and lunged at us if we got too close — which we didn't!

"Why is he so vicious?" I asked, tossing him a large chunk of raw meat, which he grabbed in midair and bit into.

"Because he's a real wolf-man," Evra said. "He's not just somebody very hairy. He's half human, half wolf."

"Isn't it cruel to keep him chained up?" I asked, throwing him another slice of meat.

"If we didn't, he'd run free and kill people. The mix of human and wolf blood has driven him mad. He wouldn't just kill when he was hungry; if he was free, he'd murder all the time."

"Isn't there a cure?" I asked, feeling sorry for him.

"There isn't a cure because it isn't a disease," Evra explained. "This isn't something he caught, it's how he was born. This is what he is."

"How did it happen?" I asked.

Evra looked at me seriously. "Do you really want to know?"

I stared at the hairy monster in the cage, ripping up the meat as if it were cotton candy, then gulped and said, "No, I suppose I don't."

We did a bunch of jobs after that. We peeled potatoes for the night's dinner, helped repair a tire on one of the cars, spent an hour painting the roof of a van, and walked a dog. Evra said most days were like this, just wandering through the camp, seeing what needed doing, helping out here and there.

In the evening we took a garbage bag full of cans and broken pieces of glass to the tent of Rhamus Twobellies, a huge man who could eat anything. I wanted to stay and watch him eat, but Evra hurried me out. Rhamus didn't like people watching him eat when he wasn't performing.

We had a lot of time to ourselves, and during our quieter moments we told each other about our lives — where we'd come from and how we'd grown up.

Evra had been born to ordinary parents. They were horrified when they saw him. They abandoned him at an orphanage, where he stayed until an evil circus owner bought him at the age of four.

"Those were bad days," he said quietly. "He used to beat me and treat me like a real snake. He kept me locked up in a glass case and let people pay to look at me and laugh."

He was with the circus for seven long, miserable years, touring small towns, being made to feel ugly and freakish and useless.

Finally, Mr. Tall came to the rescue.

"He showed up one night," Evra said. "He appeared suddenly out of the darkness and stood by my cage for a long time, watching me. He didn't say a word. Neither did I.

"The circus owner came. He didn't know who Mr. Tall was, but thought he might be a rich man, interested in buying me. He gave him his price and stood back, waiting for an answer.

"Mr. Tall didn't say anything for a few minutes.

Then his left hand grabbed the circus owner by the neck. He squeezed once and that was the end of him. He fell to the floor, dead. Mr. Tall opened the door to my cage and said, 'Let's go, Evra.' I think Mr. Tall's able to read minds, which is how he knew my name."

Evra was quiet after that. He had a faraway look in his eyes.

"Do you want to see something amazing?" he finally said, snapping out of his thoughtful mood.

"Sure," I said.

He turned to face me, then stuck out his tongue and pushed it up over his lip and *right up his nose!*

"Ewww! Gross!" I yelled delightedly.

He pulled the tongue back and grinned. "I've got the longest tongue in the world," he said. "If my nose were big enough, I could poke my tongue all the way to the top, down my throat, and back out my mouth again."

"You couldn't!" I laughed.

"Probably not." He giggled. "But it's still pretty impressive." He stuck his tongue out again and this time licked around his nostrils, one after the other. It was revolting but hilarious.

"That's the most disgusting thing I've ever seen." I laughed.

"I bet you wish you could do it," Evra said.

"I wouldn't, even if I could," I lied. "Don't you get snot all over your tongue?"

"I don't have any snot," Evra said.

"What? No snot?"

"It's true," he said. "My nose is different from yours. There's no snot or dirt or hairs. My nostrils are the cleanest part of my whole body."

"What does it taste like?" I asked.

"Lick my snake's belly and you'll find out," he replied. "It's the same taste as that."

I laughed and said I wasn't *that* interested!

Later, when Mr. Crepsley asked me what I'd done all day, I told him: "I made a friend."

CHAPTER TEN

WE'D BEEN WITH THE CIRQUE two days and nights. I spent my days helping Evra and my nights with Mr. Crepsley, learning about vampires. I was going to bed earlier than I had been, though I rarely hit the sack before one or two in the morning.

Evra and I were tight friends. He was older than me, but he was shy — probably because of his abusive childhood — so we made a good team.

As the third day rolled by, I was gazing around the small groups of vans and cars and tents, feeling like I'd been part of the scene for years.

I was starting to suffer from the effects of going for too long without drinking human blood. I wasn't as strong as I had been, and couldn't move as quickly as I could before. My eyesight had dulled, and so had my hearing and sense of smell. I was a lot stronger and quicker than I'd been as a human, but I could feel my powers slipping a little more every day.

I didn't care. I'd rather lose some strength than drink from a human.

I was relaxing with Evra on the edge of the campsite that afternoon when we spotted a figure in the bushes.

"Who's that?" I asked.

"A kid from a nearby village," Evra said. "I've seen him hanging around before."

I watched the boy in the bushes. He was trying hard not to be seen, but to someone with my powers — fading though they were — he was as obvious as an elephant. I was curious to know what he was doing, so I turned to Evra and said, "Let's have fun."

"What do you mean?" he asked.

"Lean in and I'll tell you."

I whispered my plan in his ear. He grinned and nodded, then stood and pretended to yawn.

"I'm leaving, Darren," he said. "See you later."

"See you, Evra," I replied loudly. I waited until he was gone, then stood and walked back to the camp myself.

When I was out of sight of the boy in the bushes, I went back, using the vans and tents to hide my movements. I walked about a hundred yards to the left, then crept forward until I could see the boy and sneaked toward him.

I stopped ten yards away. I was a little behind him, so he couldn't see me. His eyes were still glued to the camp. I looked over his head and saw Evra, who was even closer than I was. He made an "okay" sign with his thumb and index finger.

I crouched down low and moaned.

"Ohhhh," I groaned. "Wwwooohhhh."

The boy stiffened and looked over his shoulder nervously. He couldn't see me.

"Who's there?" he asked.

"Wraaarghhhh," Evra grunted on the other side of him.

The boy's head spun around in the other direction.

"Who's there?" he shouted.

"Ohh-ohh-ohh," I snorted, like a gorilla.

"I'm not afraid," the boy said, edging backward. "You're just somebody playing a mean trick."

"Eee-ee-ee-ee-ee," Evra screeched.

I shook a branch, Evra rattled a bush, then I tossed a stone into the area just ahead of the boy. His head was spinning around like a puppet's, darting all over the place. He didn't know whether it would be safer to run or stay.

"Look, I don't know who you are," he began, "but I'm —"

Evra snuck up behind him and now, as the boy spoke, stuck out his extra-long tongue and ran it over the boy's neck, making a hissing snake noise.

That was enough for the boy. He screamed and ran for his life.

Evra and me ran after him, laughing our heads off, making all these noises. The boy fled through thorn bushes as though they weren't there, screaming for help.

We got tired after a few minutes and would have let him get away, but then he tripped and went sprawling into a patch of really high grass.

We stood, trying to spot him in the grass, but there was no sign of him.

"Where is he?" I asked.

"I can't see him," Evra said.

"Do you think he's all right?"

"I don't know." Evra looked worried. "He might have fallen down a big hole or something."

"Kid?" I shouted. "Are you okay?" No answer. "You don't need to be afraid. We won't hurt you. We were only kidding. We didn't —"

There was a rustling noise behind us, then I felt a

hand on my back, shoving me forward into the grass. Evra fell with me. When we sat up, spluttering with shock, we heard somebody laughing behind us.

We turned around slowly, and there was the kid, doubled over with laughter.

"I got you! I got you!" he sang. "I saw you coming from the beginning. I was only pretending to be frightened. I ambushed you. Ha-ha!"

He was making fun of us, and, though we felt pretty stupid, when we stood and looked at each other we burst out laughing. He'd led us into a patch of grass filled with sticky green seeds and we were covered in them from head to foot.

"You look like a walking plant," I joked.

"*You* look like the Jolly Green Giant," Evra replied.

"Both of you look stupid," the boy said. We stared at him, and his smile faded a little. "Well, you *do*," he grumbled.

"I suppose you think this is funny," I snarled. He nodded silently. "Well, I've got news for you," I said, stepping closer, putting on the meanest face I could. I paused menacingly, then burst into a smile. "It is!"

He laughed happily, relieved that we could see the funny side of things, then stuck out his hands, one to each of us. "Hey," he said as we shook. "My name's Sam Grest. Nice to meetcha."

"Hey, Sam," I said, and as I shook his hand I thought to myself, "Looks like this is friend number two. Cool."

And Sam did become my friend. But by the time the Cirque Du Freak moved on, I was wishing with all my heart that I'd never even heard his name.

CHAPTER ELEVEN

Sam LIVED ABOUT A MILE away, with his mom and dad, two younger brothers and a baby sister, three dogs, five cats, a turtle, and a tank full of tropical fish.

"It's like living in Noah's ark," he said. "I try to stay out of the house as much as possible. Mom and Dad don't mind. They think children should be free to express their individuality. As long as I come home for bed at night, they're happy. They don't even care if I miss school every once in a while. They think school's a despotic system of indoctrination, designed to crush the spirit and stamp out creativity."

Sam talked like that all the time. He was younger than me, but you wouldn't have known it by listening to him speak.

"So, you two guys are with the show?" he asked, rolling a piece of pickled onion around his mouth —

he loved pickled onions and carried a small plastic jar of them with him. We'd returned to the spot at the edge of the clearing. Evra was lying in the grass, I was sitting on a low-hanging branch, and Sam was climbing the tree above me.

"What sort of a show is it?" he asked, before we could answer his first question. "There are no signs on your vans. At first I thought you were tourists. Then, after observing for a while, I decided you must be performers of some kind."

"We're masters of the macabre," Evra said. "Agents of mutations. Lords of the surreal." He was speaking like that to show he could match Sam's big vocabulary. I wish I could have spouted a few smarty-pants sentences, but I'd never been good with words.

"It's a magic show?" Sam asked excitedly.

"It's a freak show," I said.

"A *freak* show?" His jaw dropped open and a piece of pickled onion fell out. I had to move quickly to dodge it. "Two-headed men and weirdos like that?"

"Sort of," I said, "but our performers are magical, wonderful artists, not just people who look different."

"Cool!" He glanced at Evra. "Of course, I could see from the start that you were dermatologically challenged" — he was talking about Evra's skin (I looked the word up in a dictionary later) — "but I had no idea there might be other members like you among your company."

He looked over toward the camp, eyes bright with curiosity. "This is most fascinating." He sighed. "What other bizarre examples of the human form do your numbers include?"

"If you mean, 'What other sort of performers are there?' the answer is tons," I told him. "We have a bearded lady, of course."

"A wolf-man," Evra said.

"A man with two bellies," I added.

We went through the entire list, Evra mentioning some I'd never seen. The lineup of the Cirque Du Freak often changed. Performers came and went, depending on where the show was playing.

Sam was very impressed and, for the first time since we'd met, had nothing to say. He listened silently, eyes wide, sucking on one of his pickled onions, shaking his head once in a while as though he couldn't believe what he was hearing.

"It's so cool," he said when we finished. "You must be the luckiest guys on the planet. Living with real circus freaks, traveling the world, privy to solemn and magnificent secrets. I'd do anything to trade places with you. . . ."

I smiled to myself. I don't think he would have

liked to trade places with *me,* not if he knew the full story.

"Hey!" he said. "Could you help me join? I'm a hard worker and I'm really smart. I'd be an asset. Could I join? As an assistant? Please?"

Evra and me smiled at each other.

"I don't think so, Sam," Evra said. "We don't take on many guys our age. If you were older, or if your parents wanted to join, that would be different."

"But they wouldn't mind," Sam insisted. "They'd be delighted for me. They're always saying travel broadens the mind. They'd love the idea of me going around the world, having adventures, seeing marvelous, mystical sights."

Evra shook his head. "Sorry. Maybe when you're older."

Sam pouted and kicked some leaves off a nearby branch. They floated down over me and a few stuck in my hair.

"It's not fair," he grumbled. "People always say 'when you're older.' Where would the world be if Alexander the Great had waited until he was older? And how about Joan of Arc? If she'd waited until she was older, the English might have conquered and colonized France. Who decides when someone's old enough to make decisions for himself? It should come down to the individual."

He ranted on for a while longer, complaining about adults and the "corrupt frigging system" and about the time being ripe for a young people's revolution. It was like listening to a crazy politician on TV.

"If a kid wants to open a candy factory, let him open one," Sam stormed. "If he wants to become a football star, fine. If he wants to be an explorer and set off for strange, cannibal-populated islands, okay! We're the slaves of the modern generation. We're —"

"Sam," Evra interrupted. "Do you want to come see my snake?"

Sam broke out into a smile. "Do I?" he yelled. "I thought you'd never ask. C'mon, let's go." Leaping down out of the tree, he ran for the campsite as fast as he could, speeches forgotten. We followed slowly, laughing, feeling a whole lot older and wiser than we were.

CHAPTER TWELVE

SAM THOUGHT THE SNAKE was the coolest thing he'd ever seen. He wasn't at all scared and didn't hesitate to wrap her around his neck like a scarf. He asked a bunch of questions: How long was she, what did she eat, how often did she shed her skin, where was she from, how fast could she move?

Evra answered all of Sam's questions. He was a snake expert. There wasn't a thing he didn't know about the serpent kingdom. He was even able to tell Sam roughly how many scales the snake had!

We gave Sam a guided tour of the campsite after that. We took him to see the wolf-man (Sam was pretty quiet outside of the hairy wolf-man's van, totally frightened by the snarling creature inside). We introduced him to Hans Hands. Then we ran into Rhamus Twobellies practicing his act. Evra asked if we could watch, and Rhamus let us. Sam's eyes almost popped out of his head when he saw Rhamus chew a glass into tiny pieces, swallow it, piece it back together inside his belly, and bring it up his throat and out his mouth.

I was going to grab Madam Octa and show Sam some of the tricks I could do with her, but I didn't feel too great. The lack of human blood in my diet was getting to me; my stomach grumbled a lot, no matter how much food I ate, and I sometimes got sick or had to sit down suddenly. I didn't want to faint or get sick with the tarantula out of her cage; I knew from experience how deadly she could be if you lost control of her for even a couple of seconds.

Sam would have stayed forever, but it was getting dark and I knew Mr. Crepsley would be waking soon. Evra and me had jobs to do, so we told him it was time he went home.

"Can't I stay a little longer?" he pleaded.

"Your mother's probably looking for you for dinner," Evra said.

"I can eat with you guys," Sam said.

"There isn't enough food," I lied.

"Well, I'm not very hungry, anyway," Sam said. "I already ate most of my pickled onions."

"Maybe he could stay," Evra said. I stared at him,

CHAPTER THIRTEEN

Evra's fear went away as the evening wore on, but he was slow to return to normal and was really edgy the whole night. I had to take his knife from him and do his share when he was peeling potatoes for dinner; I was afraid he might slice one of his fingers off.

After we'd eaten and helped clean the dishes, I asked Evra about the mysterious Mr. Tiny. We were in the tent, and Evra was playing with his snake.

He didn't answer immediately, and for a while I thought he wasn't going to, but in the end he sighed and began to speak.

"Mr. Tiny is the leader of the Little People," he said.

"The small guys in the blue-hooded capes?" I asked.

"Yup. He calls them Little People. He's their boss.

He doesn't come here a lot — it's been two years since I last saw him — but he gives me the creeps when he does. He's the spookiest man I've ever met."

"He looked all right to me," I said.

"That's what I thought the first time I saw him," Evra agreed. "But wait till you've spoken to him. It's hard to explain, but every time he looks at me, I feel like he's planning to slaughter, skin, and roast me."

"He eats people?" I asked, freaked out.

"I don't know," Evra said. "Maybe he does, maybe he doesn't. But you get the feeling he *wants* to eat you. And it's not just me being stupid; I've talked about it with other members of the Cirque and they feel the same way. Nobody likes him. Even Mr. Tall gets fidgety when Mr. Tiny's around."

"Well, the Little People must like him, don't they?" I asked. "They follow and obey him, right?"

"Maybe they're scared of him," Evra said. "Maybe he forces them to obey him. Maybe they're his slaves."

"Have you ever asked them?"

"They don't talk," Evra said. "I don't know if it's because they can't or if they don't want to, but nobody in the circus has ever been able to get a word out of them. They're really helpful and they'll do whatever you ask but they're as silent as walking dummies."

"Have you ever seen their faces?" I asked.

"Once," Evra said. "Usually they don't let their hoods slip, but one day I was helping a couple of them move a heavy machine. It fell on one of the Little People and crushed him. He didn't make a sound, even though he must have been in a huge amount of pain. His hood fell to the side and I caught a glimpse of his face.

"It was disgusting," Evra said quietly, stroking the snake. "Full of scars and stitches all crumpled together, like some giant had squeezed it with his claws. He didn't have ears or a nose, and there was some kind of mask over his mouth. The skin was gray and dead-looking, and his eyes were like two green bowls near the top of his face. He didn't have hair, either."

Evra shivered at the memory. I felt cold myself, thinking about his description.

"What happened to him?" I asked. "Did he die?"

"I don't know," Evra said. "A couple of his brothers — I always think of them as brothers, though they probably aren't — came and took him away."

"You never saw him again?"

"They all look the same," Evra said. "Some are a little smaller or taller than the others, but there's no real way of telling them apart. Believe me — I've tried."

Weirder and weirder. I was really intrigued by Mr.

Tiny and his Little People. I'd always liked mysteries. Maybe I could solve this one. Maybe, with my vampire powers, I could find a way to talk to one of the hooded creatures.

"Where do the Little People come from?" I asked.

"Nobody knows," Evra said. "There's usually about four or six of them with the Cirque. Sometimes more turn up by themselves. Sometimes Mr. Tiny brings in new ones. It was weird that none were here when you came."

"You think it had something to do with me and Mr. Crepsley coming?" I asked.

"I doubt it," Evra said. "It was probably just a coincidence. Or fate." He paused. "Which is another thing: Mr. Tiny's first name is Desmond."

"So?"

"He tells people to call him Des."

"So?" I asked again.

"Put it together with his last name," Evra told me.

I did. Mr. Des Tiny. Mr. Des-Tiny. Mr. . . .

"Mr. Destiny," I whispered, and Evra nodded seriously.

I was dying of curiosity and asked Evra a bunch more questions, but his answers were limited. He knew almost nothing about Mr. Tiny, and only a little more about the Little People. They ate meat. They smelled funny. They moved around slowly most of the time. They either didn't feel pain or couldn't show it. And they had no sense of humor.

"How do you know that?" I asked.

"Bradley Stretch," Evra answered darkly. "He used to be with the show. He had rubbery bones and could make his arms and legs stretch.

"He wasn't very nice. He was always playing practical jokes on us, and he had a nasty way of laughing. He didn't just make you look like an idiot: He made you feel like one too.

"We played a show in an Arabian palace. It was a private show for a sheik. He enjoyed all the acts, but especially liked Bradley's. The two started talking, and Bradley told the sheik he couldn't wear jewelry, because it always slipped off or broke because of the changing shape of his body.

"The sheik ran away and came back with a small gold bracelet. He gave it to Bradley and told him to put it on his wrist. Bradley did. Then the sheik told him to try shaking it off.

"So Bradley made his arm small and big, short and long, but he couldn't shake the bracelet loose. The sheik said it was magic and could only be removed if the wearer wanted to take it off. It was really valuable, priceless, but he gave it to Bradley as a gift.

"Getting back to the Little People," Evra said. "Bradley loved to tease them. He was always finding new ways to trick them. He made traps to hang them up in the air by their feet. He set their capes on fire. He squirted liquid laundry detergent on ropes they were using to make their hands slip, or glue to make them stick. He put thumbtacks in their food and he made their tent collapse and locked them in a van."

"Why was he so mean?" I asked.

"I think because they never reacted," Evra said. "He liked to see people get upset, but the Little People never cried or screamed or lashed out. They didn't seem to notice his pranks. At least, everybody *thought* they didn't notice. . . ."

Evra made a funny noise that was half a laugh, half a moan.

"One morning we woke up and Bradley had disappeared. Nowhere to be found. We searched for him, but when he didn't turn up, we moved on. We weren't worried; performers join and leave the Cirque pretty much as they please. It wasn't the first time somebody had sneaked away in the middle of the night.

"I didn't think any more about it until a week or so later. Mr. Tiny had come to see us the day before and took all but two of the Little People with him. Mr. Tall told me I had to help the leftover pair with their duties. I cleaned up their tent and rolled up their hammocks — they all sleep in hammocks. That's where I got mine from. Did I mention that before?" He hadn't, but I didn't want to sidetrack him, so I said nothing.

"After that," he went on, "I washed their pot. It was a big black pot, set on a fire in the middle of the tent. The place had to have been full of smoke whenever they cooked because the pot was covered in grime.

"I took it outside and tried to scrape the grime — scraps of meat and pieces of bone — onto the grass. I scrubbed it thoroughly, then took it back inside. Next I decided to pick up the pieces of meat in the grass and throw them to the wolf-man. 'Waste not, want not,' like Mr. Tall always says.

"As I was picking up the meat and bone, I saw something glistening. . . ."

Evra turned away and rifled through a bag on the ground. When he turned back, he was holding a small gold bracelet. He let my eyes linger on it, then slipped it on over his left hand. He shook his arm as fast as he could but the bracelet never moved.

When he stopped shaking his arm, he slid the bracelet off with the fingers of his right hand and tossed it to me. I examined it but didn't put it on.

"The bracelet the sheik gave to Bradley Stretch?" I guessed.

"The same," Evra said.

I handed it back.

"I don't know whether it was because of something really bad he did," Evra said, fingering the bracelet, "or if they were just tired of the nonstop teasing. What I do know is, ever since, I've gone out of my way to be polite to the small, silent people in the dark blue capes."

"What did you do with the remains of . . . I mean, with the scraps of meat?" I asked. "Did you bury them?"

"Heck, no," Evra said. "I fed them to the wolfman, like I meant to." Then, in response to my horrified look, he said, "Waste not, want not, remember?"

I stared at him for a second, then began to laugh. Evra laughed, too. In a minute we were both rolling around on the floor in hysterics.

"We shouldn't laugh." I caught my breath. "Poor Bradley Stretch. We should be crying."

"I'm laughing too hard to cry," Evra gasped.

"I wonder what he tasted like?"

"I don't know," Evra said. "But I bet he was rubbery."

That made us laugh even more. Tears rolled from

our eyes and trickled down our cheeks. It was a terrible thing to laugh at, but we couldn't help it.

In the middle of our fit of hysteria, the flap to the door of our tent was pulled aside by an inquisitive head, and Hans Hands entered. "What's the joke?" he asked, but we couldn't tell him. I tried, but every time I started, I began to laugh again.

He shook his head and rolled his eyes. Then, when we finally quieted down, he told us why he was there.

"I have a message for you two," he said. "Mr. Tall wants you to report to his van as soon as possible."

"What's up, Hans?" Evra asked. He was still laughing. "Why does he want us?"

"He doesn't," Hans said. "Mr. Tiny is with him. *He's* the one who wants you."

Our laughter stopped instantly. Hans let himself out without any further words.

"Mr. Tuh-tuh-tuh-Tiny wants us," Evra gasped.

"I heard," I said. "What do you think he wants?"

"I don't kn-kn-kn-know," Evra stuttered, though I could tell what was going through his mind. It was the same thing that was rushing through mine. We were thinking of the Little People, Bradley Stretch, and the big black pot full of scraps of human meat and bone.

CHAPTER FOURTEEN

MR. TALL, MR. CREPSLEY, and Mr. Tiny were in the van when we entered. Evra was shaking like a leaf, but I wasn't really nervous. But when I saw the worried looks on Mr. Tall's and Mr. Crepsley's faces and realized how uneasy they were, it put me on edge a little.

"Come in, boys," Mr. Tiny welcomed us, as though it was his van and not Mr. Tall's. "Sit down, make yourselves at home."

"I'll stand if that's okay," Evra said, trying not to let us hear the chatter of his teeth.

"I'll stand, too," I said, following Evra's lead.

"As you wish," Mr. Tiny said. He was the only one sitting.

"I've been hearing a lot about you, young Darren Shan," Mr. Tiny said. He was rolling something between his hands: a heart-shaped watch. I could hear it ticking whenever there was a pause in his speech.

"You're quite the boy, by all accounts," Mr. Tiny went on. "A most remarkable young man. Sacrificed everything to save a friend. There aren't many who would do as much. People are so self-centered these days. It's good to see the world can still produce heroes."

"I'm no hero," I said, blushing at the compliment.

"Of course you are," he insisted. "What is a hero but a person who lays everything on the line for the good of somebody else?"

I smiled proudly. I couldn't understand why Evra was so afraid of this nice, strange man. There was nothing terrible about Mr. Tiny. I kind of liked him.

"Larten tells me you're reluctant to drink human blood," Mr. Tiny continued. "I don't blame you. Nasty, repulsive stuff. Can't stand it. Apart from young children, of course. Their blood is scrump-dilly-icious."

I frowned. "You can't drink blood from them," I said. "They're too small. If you took blood from a young child, you'd kill it."

His eyes widened and so did his smile.

"*So?*" he asked softly.

A chill ran down my spine. If he had been joking, it would have been in really poor taste, but I could have overlooked it (hadn't I just been laughing about poor Bradley Stretch?). But I could tell from his expression that he was totally serious.

All of a sudden I knew why this man was so feared. *He was evil.* Not just bad or nasty, but pure demonic evil. This was a man I could imagine killing thousands of people just to hear them scream.

"You know," Mr. Tiny said, "your face seems familiar. Have we met before, Darren Shan?"

I shook my head.

"Are you certain?" he asked. "You look *very* familiar."

"I . . . would have . . . remembered," I stuttered.

"You can't always trust memory." Mr. Tiny smiled. "It can be a deceptive monster. Still, no matter. Maybe I'm confusing you with someone else."

By the way his lips twisted into a grin (how did I ever think that was a nice smile?), I could see he didn't think that. But I was sure he was wrong. There's no way I would have forgotten meeting a creature like him.

"Down to business," Mr. Tiny said. His hands tightened on the heart-shaped watch and for a second they seemed to glow and melt into its ticking face. I blinked and rubbed my eyes. When I looked again, the illusion — which it must have been — was gone.

"You boys saw me arrive with my Little People," Mr. Tiny said. "They're new converts to my cause and are a little unsure of the ropes. Normally I'd stick around and teach them how to work, but I have business elsewhere. Still, they're smart and I'm sure they'll learn.

"However, while they're learning, I'd like it if you two fine, young men would help ease them into the swing of things. You won't have to do much. Mainly I want you to find food for them. They have such big appetites.

"How about it, boys? I've got the permission of your guardians." He nodded at Mr. Tall and Mr. Crepsley, who didn't seem happy about the arrangement, but looked resigned. "Will you help poor old Mr. Tiny and his Little People?"

I looked at Evra. I could see he didn't want to do it, but he nodded his head anyway. I did the same.

"Excellent!" Mr. Tiny boomed. "Young Evra Von knows what my darlings like, I'm sure. If you have any problems, report to Hibernius and he'll help you out."

Mr. Tiny waved a hand to let us know we could

leave. Evra began edging backward immediately, but I held my ground.

"Excuse me," I said, summoning all my courage, "but why do you call them Little People?"

Mr. Tiny turned around slowly. If he was surprised by my question, he didn't show it, though I could see the mouths of Mr. Tall and Mr. Crepsley dropping.

"Because they're little," he explained calmly.

"I know that," I said. "But don't they have another name? An official name? If somebody mentioned 'Little People' to me, I'd think they were talking about elves or leprechauns."

Mr. Tiny smiled. "They *are* elves and leprechauns," he said. "All around the world, you will find legends and stories of small, magical people. Legends have to start somewhere. These legends started with my short, loyal friends."

"Are you telling me those dwarfs in blue capes are *elves?*" I asked disbelievingly.

"No," he said. "Elves don't exist. Those dwarfs — as you so rudely put it — were seen, long ago, by ignorant people, who invented names for them: elves or fairies or sprites. They made up stories about what they were and what they could do."

"What *can* they do?" I asked.

Mr. Tiny's smile slipped. "I heard you were quite the one for asking questions," he growled, "but nobody told me you were *this* nosy. Remember, Darren Shan: Curiosity killed the cat."

"I'm not a cat," I said boldly.

Mr. Tiny leaned forward, and his face darkened. "If you ask more questions," he hissed, "you might find yourself turned into one. Nothing in life is forever, not even the human form."

The watch in his hands glowed again, red like a real heart, and I decided it was time to leave.

"Go to bed now and get a good night's sleep," Mr. Crepsley told me before I left. "There will be no lessons tonight."

"And rise early, boys," Mr. Tiny added, waving goodbye. "My Little People are always hungry in the mornings. It's not wise to let their hunger go unattended. You never know what they might set their minds — and *teeth* — on if they go unfed for too long."

We hurried out the door and raced back to our tent, where we fell to the floor and listened to our hearts beating loudly.

"Are you crazy?" Evra asked when he could speak. "Talking to Mr. Tiny like that, asking him questions, you must be out of your mind!"

"You're right," I said, thinking back on the encounter, wondering where I'd gotten the nerve from. "I must be."

Evra shook his head in disgust. It was early, but we crawled into bed anyway. We lay awake for hours, staring at the ceiling of the tent. When I finally fell asleep I dreamed of Mr. Tiny and his heart-shaped watch. Only, in my dreams, it wasn't a watch. It was a real human heart. *Mine.* And when he squeezed it . . .

Agony.

CHAPTER FIFTEEN

WE GOT UP EARLY and went hunting for food for the Little People. We were tired and cranky, and it took time for us to come to life.

After a while I asked Evra what the Little People liked to eat.

"Meat," he replied. "Any kind of animal, they don't care."

"How many animals will we need to catch?" I asked.

"Well, there's twelve of them, but they don't eat a lot. I guess one rabbit or hedgehog between two of them. A larger animal — a fox or a dog — might feed three or four."

"Can you eat hedgehogs?" I asked.

"The Little People can," Evra said. "They're not fussy. They'd eat rats and mice, too, but we'd have to catch a lot to feed so many, so they're not worth bothering with."

We each took a sack and headed off in different directions. Evra told me the meat didn't have to be fresh, so if I found a dead badger or squirrel, I could stick it in the bag and save some time.

I spotted a fox a couple of minutes into the hunt. It had a chicken in its mouth and was on its way home. I tracked it until the moment was right, then jumped on it from behind a bush and dragged it to the ground.

The dead chicken flew out of its mouth and the fox turned, snarling, to bite me. Before it could attack, I moved quickly, grabbed its neck, and twisted sharply to the left. There was a loud crack, and that was the end of the fox.

I chucked the chicken into the bag — a nice bonus — but hung on to the fox for a few minutes. I needed blood, so I found a vein, made a small cut, and started sucking.

Part of me hated this — it seemed so inhuman — but I reminded myself that I *wasn't* human anymore. I was a half-vampire. This was how my kind acted. I'd felt bad killing foxes and rabbits and pigs and sheep the first few times. But I got used to it. I had to.

Could I get used to drinking human blood? That was the question. I hoped I could avoid feeding on humans, but by the way I was running out of energy, I knew eventually I'd have to . . . or die.

I tossed the fox's corpse into the bag, then went on hunting. I found a family of rabbits washing their ears in a nearby pond. I crept as close as I could, then struck without warning. They scattered in fear, but not before I got my sharp fingernails into three of the little ones.

I added them to the contents of the bag and decided that was enough for this trip. I figured the fox, chicken, and rabbits would easily feed six or seven of the blue-hoods.

I met Evra back at camp. He'd found a dead dog and a badger and was feeling pretty pleased with himself. "The easiest day of hunting I've ever had," he said. "Plus I found a field full of cows. We'll go there tonight and steal one. That'll keep the Little People going for a day or two at least."

"Won't the farmer who owns them notice?" I asked.

"There are at least a hundred of them," Evra said. "By the time he gets around to counting them, we'll be long gone."

"But cows cost money," I said. "I don't mind killing wild animals, but stealing from a farmer is different."

"We'll leave money for him," Evra said with a sigh.

"Where will we get it?" I asked.

Evra smiled. "The one thing we're never short of at the Cirque Du Freak is money," he assured me.

Later, our chores finished, we teamed up with Sam again. He'd been waiting in the bushes for hours.

"Why didn't you come into the camp?" I asked.

"I didn't want to interrupt," he said. "Besides, I thought somebody might have let the wolf-man out. He didn't seem to like me when I saw him yesterday."

"He's like that with everyone," Evra told him.

"Maybe," Sam said, "but I figure it's best not to take chances."

Sam was in a questioning mood. He'd obviously been thinking about us a lot since the day before.

"Don't you ever wear shoes?" he asked Evra.

"No," Evra said. "The soles of my feet are extra tough."

"What happens if you step on a thorn or a nail?" Sam asked.

Evra smiled, sat down, and gave Sam his foot. "Try scratching it with a sharp twig," he said.

Sam broke off a branch and poked Evra's sole. It was like trying to make a hole in tough leather.

"A sharp piece of glass might slice me," Evra said,

"but that doesn't happen very often, and my skin's getting tougher every year."

"I wish I had skin like that," Sam said enviously. Then he turned to me. "How come you wear the same suit all the time?" he asked.

I looked down at the suit I'd been buried alive in. I'd meant to ask for some new clothes but had forgotten.

"I like it," I said.

"I've never seen a kid wearing a suit like that before," Sam said. "Not unless they were at a wedding or a funeral. Are you forced to wear it?"

"No," I said.

"Did you ask your parents if you could join the Cirque?" Evra said then, to distract Sam's attention.

"No," Sam sighed. "I told them about it, of course, but I figured it would be best to take it slowly. I won't tell them until just before I leave, or maybe not until I'm gone."

"So you still plan to join?" I asked.

"You bet!" Sam said. "I know you tried scaring me away, but I'll get in somehow. You wait. I'll keep coming around. I'll read books and learn everything there is to know about freak shows, and then I'll go to your boss and state my case. He won't be able to turn me down."

Evra and I smiled at each other. We knew Sam's dream would never lead to anything, but we didn't have the heart to tell him.

We went to see an old, deserted railroad station, about two miles away, which Sam had told us about.

"It's great," he said. "They used to work on trains there, repair and paint them and stuff like that. It was a busy station when it was open. Then a new station opened closer to the city and this place went bankrupt. It's a great place to play. There are rusty old railroad tracks, empty sheds, a guardhouse, and a couple of ancient train cars."

"Is it safe?" Evra asked.

"My mother says it isn't," Sam told us. "It's one of the few places she tells me to stay away from. She says I could fall through the roof of one of the cars or trip on a rail or something. But I've been there lots of times and nothing's ever happened."

It was another sunny day, and we were walking slowly under the shade of the trees when I smelled something strange. I stopped and sniffed the air. Evra could smell it, too.

"What is that?" I asked.

"I don't know," he said, sniffing the air next to me. "Which way is it coming from?"

"I can't tell," I said. It was a thick, heavy, sour smell.

Sam hadn't smelled anything and kept walking ahead of us. Then he realized we weren't beside him, stopped, and turned to see what was going on.

"What's wrong?" he asked. "Why aren't you —"

"*Gotcha!*" a voice yelled behind me, and before I could move I felt a firm hand grab my shoulder and spin me around. I saw a large, hairy face, and then suddenly I was falling backward, thrown off-balance by the force of the hand.

CHAPTER SIXTEEN

I FELL HARD ON THE GROUND and sprained my arm. I screamed with pain, then tried twisting away from the hairy figure above me. Before I could do anything, he was crouching by my side with a fierce look on his face.

"Oh, hey, man, I didn't hurt you, did I?" He had a friendly voice, and I realized my life wasn't in danger; the look on his face was one of concern, not anger.

"I didn't mean to freak you out," the man said. "I was just trying to scare you a little, man, for fun."

I sat up and rubbed my elbow. "I'm okay," I said.

"You're sure? It ain't broken, is it? I've got herbs that can help, if it is."

"Herbs can't fix broken bones," Sam said. He was now standing beside Evra.

"They sure can't," the stranger agreed, "but they can elevate you to planes of consciousness where worldly concerns like broken bones are nothing but minor blips on the cosmic map." He paused and stroked his beard. "Of course, they burn out your brain cells, too. . . ."

Sam's blank face showed that even *he* didn't understand that long sentence.

"I'm okay," I said again. I stood up and rotated my arm. "I just twisted it. It'll be fine in a couple of minutes."

"Man, that's good to hear," the stranger said. "I'd hate to be the cause of bodily harm. Hurt's a bad trip, man."

I studied him in more detail. He was big and chubby, with a bushy black beard and long, scraggly hair. His clothes were dirty and there was no way he'd had a bath recently, because he stank to high heaven. That's what the strange smell had been. He was really friendly looking; it made me feel stupid thinking about how afraid of him I'd been.

"Are you guys locals?" the man asked.

"I am," Sam said. "These guys are with the circus."

"Circus?" The man smiled. "There's a circus around here? Oh, man, how did I miss it? Where is it?

I love the circus. I never pass up a chance to see clowns in action."

"It's not that sort of circus," Sam told him. "It's a freak show."

"A freak show?" The man stared at Sam, then at Evra, whose scales and color pretty much marked him out as one of the performers. "Are you part of a freak show, man?" he asked.

Evra nodded shyly.

"They don't mistreat you, do they?" the man asked. "They don't whip you or under-feed you or make you do things you don't want to?"

"No." Evra shook his head.

"You're there of your own free will?"

"Yes," Evra said. "All of us are. It's our home."

"Oh. Well, that's okay," the man said, smiling again. "You hear rumors about those small traveling shows. You . . ." He slapped his forehead. "Oh man, I haven't introduced myself, have I? I'm so dumb sometimes. R.V.'s the name."

"R.V.? That's a funny name," I remarked.

He coughed with embarrassment. "Well," he said, lowering his voice to a whisper, "it's short for Reggie Veggie."

"*Reggie Veggie?*" I laughed.

"Yeah," he said. "Reggie's my real name. Reggie

Veggie's what they called me in school, because I'm a vegetarian. Well, I never liked that, so I asked them to call me R.V. instead. Some did, but not many." He looked miserable at the memory. "You can call me Reggie Veggie if you want," he told us.

"R.V. is fine by me," I assured him.

"Me, too," Evra said.

"And me," Sam added.

"Cool!" R.V. brightened up. "So, that's my name out in the open. How about you three?"

"Darren Shan," I told him, and we shook hands.

"Sam Grest."

"Evra Von."

"Evra Von what?" R.V. asked, as I had when I first met Evra.

"Just plain Von," Evra said.

"Oh." R.V. smiled. "Cool!"

R.V. was an ecowarrior, here to stop a road from being built. He was a member of NOP — Nature's Opposing Protectors — and had traveled the country saving forests and lakes and animals and stuff like that.

He offered to show us around his camp, and we jumped at the chance. The railway station could wait. This was an opportunity that wouldn't come every day.

He talked about the environment nonstop as we

full-length again. Cormac held it rigidly in place a few seconds longer, then flexed it in and out to show it was as good as new.

The crowd cheered, and I felt my heart slow back down to normal.

I looked down at the ground, where I'd spat out the finger, and saw it beginning to rot. Within a minute it was nothing more than a grayish mound of mold.

"Sorry if I frightened you," Cormac said, giving my head a pat.

"That's okay," I told him. "I should have learned by now to expect the unexpected around here. Can I feel the new finger?" He nodded. It didn't feel different from any of the others. "How do you do it?" I asked, amazed. "It is an illusion?"

"No illusion," he said. "It's why they call me Cormac *Limbs*. I've been able to grow new limbs — fingers, toes, arms, legs — ever since I was a toddler. My parents discovered my talent when I had an accident with a kitchen knife and cut off part of my nose. I can grow back virtually any part of my body. Except my head. I haven't tried cutting that off. I guess it's best not to tempt fate."

"Doesn't it hurt?" I asked.

"A little," he said, "but not much. When one of my limbs gets cut off, a new one starts to grow almost immediately, so there's only a second or two of pain. It's a little like —"

"Come, come!" Mr. Tall bellowed, cutting him short. "We don't have time for detailed description. This show has been idle far too long. It's time we entertained the public again, before they forget about us or think we've retired.

"People," he shouted to the crowd, and clapped his hands together. "Spread the word. The lull is over. The show goes on tonight!"

CHAPTER EIGHTEEN

THE CAMP WAS BUZZING with activity all afternoon. People were running around like crazy. A bunch of them were working on putting together the circus tent. I hadn't seen it before. It was an impressive sight when it was done, tall and round and red, decorated with pictures of the performers.

Evra and me were kept busy, hammering pegs into the ground to hold the tent in place, arranging seats inside, setting up the stage for the show, preparing props for the performers (we had to find tin cans and nuts and bolts for Rhamus Twobellies to eat, and help move the wolf-man's cage inside the tent, and so on).

It was a huge operation, but it moved with incredible speed. Everyone in the camp knew their place and what was expected of them, and there was never any real panic over the course of the day. Everybody worked as part of a team and things came together smoothly.

Sam showed up early in the afternoon. I would have kept him around to help with the work, but Evra said he'd be in the way, so we told him he had to take off. He was upset and slouched off, kicking an empty soda can along in front of him. I felt sorry for him, then realized how I could cheer him up.

"Sam! Wait a minute!" I shouted. "I'll be back in a second," I told Evra, then rushed off to Mr. Tall's van.

I knocked once on the door and it opened instantly. Mr. Tall was standing inside, and before I could say a word, he held out two tickets for entry to the Cirque Du Freak.

I stared at the tickets, then at Mr. Tall. "How did you know . . . ?"

"I have my ways," he replied with a smile.

"I don't have any money," I warned him.

"I'll take it out of your wages," he said.

I frowned. "You don't pay me anything."

His smile widened. "Clever old me." He handed over the tickets and closed the door in my face before I could thank him.

I hurried back to Sam and gave him the tickets.

"What are these?" he asked.

"Tickets for tonight's show," I told him. "One for you and one for R.V."

"Oh, wow!" Sam quickly stuck the tickets in his pocket, as if he was afraid they might blow away or vanish. "Thanks, Darren."

"No problem," I said. "The only thing is, it's a late show. We're starting at eleven, and it won't be over till nearly one in the morning. Will you be able to come?"

"Sure," Sam said. "I'll sneak out. Mom and Dad go to bed at nine every night. They're early birds."

"If you get caught," I warned him, "don't tell them where you're going."

"My lips are sealed," he promised, then set off to find R.V.

Except for a quick dinner, there was no other break between then and the start of the show. While Evra left to feed his snake, I set up candles inside the circus tent. There were also five huge chandeliers to be hung, four above the crowd and one over the stage, but the Little People took care of those.

Mags — a pretty woman who sold souvenirs and candy during intermission — asked me to help her get the displays ready, so I spent an hour stacking candy spiderwebs and edible "glass" statues and pieces of the wolf-man's hair. There was a new novelty I hadn't seen before: a small model of Cormac Limbs. When you cut a part of it off, a new piece grew in its place. I asked Mags how it worked but she didn't know.

"It's one of Mr. Tall's inventions," she said. "He makes a lot of this stuff himself."

I chopped the head off the model and tried peering down the neck to see what was inside, but a new head grew before I could.

"The models don't last forever," Mags said. "They rot after a few months."

"Do you tell people that when they're buying them?" I asked.

"Of course," she said. "Mr. Tall insists we let the customers know exactly what they're buying. He doesn't approve of conning people."

Mr. Crepsley summoned me half an hour before the show began. He was dressing in his stage costume when I entered.

"Polish Madam Octa's cage," he ordered, "then brush your suit down and clean yourself up."

"Why?" I asked.

"You are going on with me," he said.

My eyes lit up. "You mean I'm part of the act?" I gasped.

"A small part," he said. "You can bring the cage

on and play the flute when it is Madam Octa's time to spin a web over my mouth."

"Mr. Tall normally does that, doesn't he?"

"Normally," Mr. Crepsley agreed, "but we are short on performers tonight, so he is going to be performing himself. Besides, you are better suited to assisting than him."

"How so?" I asked.

"You look creepier," he said. "With your pale face and that awful suit, you look like something out of a horror film."

That gave me a little bit of a shock. I'd never thought I was creepy looking! I looked in a mirror and realized I did look sort of frightening. Because I hadn't drank human blood, I was a lot paler than I should have been. The dirty suit made me look even more ghostlike. I made up my mind to find something new to wear in the morning.

The show started at exactly eleven. I didn't expect much of a crowd — we were in the middle of nowhere and hadn't had much time to notify people about the show — but the tent was packed.

"Where did they all come from?" I whispered to Evra as we watched Mr. Tall introduce the wolf-man.

"Everywhere," he replied quietly. "People always

know when one of our shows is happening. Besides, even though he only told us about it today, Mr. Tall probably knew we'd be playing tonight ever since we set up camp."

I watched the show from the wings, enjoying it even more than the first time I'd seen it, because now I knew the people involved and felt like part of the family.

Hans Hands went on after the wolf-man, followed by Rhamus Twobellies. We had our first break, then Mr. Tall went onstage and darted around the place, never seeming to move, just vanishing from one spot and appearing somewhere new. Next up was Truska, then it was my turn to go onstage with Mr. Crepsley and Madam Octa.

The lights were low, but my vampire vision helped me pick out Sam's and R.V.'s faces in the crowd. They were surprised to see me and clapped louder than anybody else. I had to hide my excited smile: Mr. Crepsley had told me to look miserable and glum, to impress the crowd.

I stood over on one side as Mr. Crepsley made a speech about how deadly Madam Octa was, then opened the door to her cage as an assistant led a goat on the stage.

There was a loud, angry gasp when Madam Octa killed the goat . . . it came from R.V. I knew then that I shouldn't have invited him — I'd forgotten how fond he was of animals — but it was too late to take back my invitation.

I was pretty nervous when it was my turn to play the flute and control Madam Octa, feeling every set of eyes in the tent focus on me. I'd never performed for a crowd before and for a few seconds I was afraid my lips wouldn't work or I'd forget the tune. But once I started blowing and sending my thoughts to Madam Octa, I did okay.

As she weaved her web across Mr. Crepsley's lips, it struck me that I could get rid of him now if I wanted. *I could make her bite him.*

The idea shocked me. I'd thought about killing him before, but never seriously, and not since we'd joined the Cirque. Now here he was, his life in my hands. All it would take was one "slip." I could say it was an accident. Nobody would be able to prove otherwise.

I watched the spider move back and forth, up and down, her poisonous fangs glinting under the lights of the chandelier. The heat from the candles was intense. I was sweating a lot. It occurred to me that I could blame the slip of my fingers on the sweat.

Over his mouth she spun her web. His hands were down by his sides. He wouldn't be able to stop her. One wrong toot on the flute was all it would take. One broken note to stop the train of thought between the two of us, and . . .

I didn't do it. I played perfectly and safely. I wasn't sure why I spared the vampire. Maybe because Mr. Tall might know I'd killed him. Maybe because I needed Mr. Crepsley to teach me how to survive. Maybe because I didn't want to become a killer.

Or maybe, just maybe, because I was starting to like the vampire. After all, he'd brought me to the Cirque and made me part of his act. I wouldn't have met Evra and Sam if it hadn't been for him. He'd been kind to me, as kind as he could be.

Whatever the reason, I didn't let Madam Octa kill her master, and at the end of the act we took our bows and exited together.

"You thought about killing me," Mr. Crepsley said softly once we were backstage.

"What do you mean?" I played dumb.

"You know what I mean," he said. There was a pause. "It would not have worked. I milked most of the poison from her fangs before we went on. Killing the goat took the rest out of her."

"It was a test?" I stared at him, and my hatred

grew again. "I thought you were being nice to me!" I cried. "And all the time it was just a test!"

His face was serious. "I had to know," he said. "I had to know if I could rely on you."

"Well, listen to this," I growled, standing on my toes so I could go eyeball to eyeball with him. "Your test was useless. I didn't kill you this time, but if I ever get the chance again, I'll take it!"

I stormed off without another word, too upset to stick around to see Cormac Limbs or the end of the show, feeling betrayed, even though deep down I knew what he said made sense.

CHAPTER NINETEEN

I WAS STILL UPSET the next morning. Evra kept asking me what was wrong, but I wouldn't tell him. I didn't want him to know I'd been thinking of killing Mr. Crepsley.

Evra told me he'd met Sam and R.V. after the show. "Sam loved it," Evra said, "especially Cormac Limbs. You should have stayed to see Cormac in action. When he sawed his legs off . . ."

"I'll see him next time," I said. "How did R.V. take it?"

Evra frowned. "He wasn't happy."

"Upset about the goat?" I asked.

"Yeah," Evra said, "but not just that. I said we bought the goat from a butcher, so it would have been killed anyway. It was the wolf-man, the snake, and Mr. Crepsley's spider that bothered him the most."

"What was wrong with *them?*" I asked.

"He was afraid they weren't being treated right. He didn't like the idea of them being locked in cages. I told him they weren't, except for the spider. I said the wolf-man was really quiet offstage. And I showed him my snake and how she slept with me."

"Did he believe you about the wolf-man?" I asked.

"I think so," Evra said, "although he still seemed suspicious when they were leaving. And he was *very* interested in their eating habits. He wanted to know what we fed them, how often, and where we got the food. We have to be careful with R.V. He could cause problems. Luckily, he should be leaving in a day or two, but until then, beware."

The day went by quietly. Sam didn't show up until later on in the afternoon, and none of us was in the mood for playing. It was a cloudy day, and we were all a little out of sorts. Sam only stayed for half an hour, then went home again.

Mr. Crepsley summoned me to his van a little after sunset. I wasn't going to go, but decided it was best not to annoy him too much. He was my guardian, after all, and could probably have me booted out of the Cirque Du Freak.

"What do you want?" I snapped when I arrived.

"Stand over here, where I can see you better," the vampire said.

He tilted my head backward with his bony fingers and rolled up my eyelids to check the whites of my eyes. He told me to open my mouth and peered down my throat. Then he checked my pulse and reflexes.

"How do you feel?" he asked.

"Tired," I said.

"Weak?" he asked. "Sick?"

"A bit."

He grunted. "Have you been drinking much blood lately?" he asked.

"As much as I'm supposed to," I said.

"But no human blood?"

"No," I said softly.

"Okay," he said. "Get ready. We are going out."

"Hunting?" I asked.

He shook his head. "To see a friend."

I got up on his back outside the van, and he began running.

When we were far enough away from the camp, he flitted and the world blurred around us.

I didn't really pay attention to where we were going. I was more concerned with my suit. I'd forgotten to get new clothes, and now, the more I examined it, the worse the suit seemed.

There were dozens of small holes and rips, and the color was a lot grayer than it was supposed to be, because of the dirt and dust. Strands of thread and fibers had come loose, and every time I shook an arm or a leg I looked like I was shedding hairs.

I'd never been very worried about clothes, but I didn't want to look like a *bum*. Tomorrow I'd definitely find something new to wear.

After a while we approached a city and Mr. Crepsley slowed down. He stopped outside the back of a tall building. I wanted to ask where we were, but he put a finger to his lips and made the sign for silence.

The back door was locked but Mr. Crepsley laid a hand over it and clicked the fingers of his other hand. It opened instantly. He led the way through a long, dark corridor, then up a set of stairs and into a brightly lit hallway.

After a few minutes, we came to a white desk. Mr. Crepsley looked around to make sure we were alone, then rang the bell that hung from one of the walls.

A figure appeared behind the glass wall on the other side of the desk. The door in the glass wall opened and a brown-haired man in a white uniform and green mask stepped through. He looked like a doctor.

"How may I — ," he began, then stopped. "Larten Crepsley! What are you doing here, you old devil?"

The man pulled down his mask, and I saw he was grinning.

"Hello, Jimmy," Mr. Crepsley said. The two shook hands and smiled at each other. "Long time no see."

"Not as long as I thought it would be," the man called Jimmy said. "I heard you'd been killed. An old enemy finally rammed a stake through your rotten heart, or so the story went."

"You should not believe everything you hear," Mr. Crepsley said. He put a hand on my shoulder and nudged me forward. "Jimmy, this is Darren Shan, a traveling companion of mine. Darren, this is Jimmy Ovo, an old friend and the world's finest pathologist."

"Hello," I said.

"Pleased to meet you," Jimmy said, shaking my hand. "You aren't a . . . I mean, do you belong to *the club?*"

"He is a vampire," Mr. Crepsley said.

"Only half of me," I snapped. "I'm not a full vampire."

"Please," Jimmy winced. "Don't use that word. I know what you guys are, and I'm fine with it, but that 'V' word never fails to freak me out." He shivered playfully. "I think it's because of all the horror movies I watched when I was a kid. I know you're not like those movie monsters, but it's hard to get the image out of my mind."

"What's a pathologist do?" I asked.

"I cut corpses open to see how they died," Jimmy explained. "I don't do it with a lot of bodies — just the ones who died in suspicious circumstances."

"This is a city morgue," Mr. Crepsley said. "They store bodies that arrive dead at the hospital or die while they're there."

"Is that where you keep them?" I asked Jimmy, pointing at the room behind the glass wall.

"Yup," he said cheerfully. He swung up a section of the desk and invited us through.

I was nervous. I expected to see dozens of tables piled high with sliced-open bodies. But it wasn't like that. There was one dead body, covered from head to toe with a long sheet, but that was the only one I could see. Otherwise it was a huge, well-lit room, with big filing cabinets built in the walls and lots of medical equipment scattered around the place.

"How is business?" Mr. Crepsley asked as we sat on three chairs near the corpse on the table. Jimmy and Mr. Crepsley didn't pay attention to the dead person, and since I didn't want to look out of place, neither did I.

"Slow enough," Jimmy answered. "The weather's been good, and there haven't been many car accidents. No strange diseases, no food epidemics, no collapsing buildings. By the way," he added, "I had an old friend of yours in here a few years back."

"Oh?" Mr. Crepsley responded politely. "Who was that?"

Jimmy sniffed heavily through his nose, then cleared his throat.

"*Gavner Purl?*" Mr. Crepsley hooted with delight. "How is the old dog — as clumsy as ever?"

They started talking about their friend Gavner Purl. I looked around while they were speaking, wondering where the bodies were kept. Finally, when they paused for breath, I asked Jimmy. He stood up, and told me to follow. He led the way to the big filing cabinets and pulled one of the drawers out.

There was a hissing sound, and a cloud of cold air rose from inside the drawer. When it cleared, I saw a sheet-covered form and realized the filing cabinets weren't filing cabinets at all. They were refrigerated coffins!

"We store the bodies here until we're ready,"

Jimmy said, "or until their next of kin come to collect them."

I looked around the room, counting the rows of drawer doors. "Is there a body behind each of these?" I asked.

Jimmy shook his head. "We've only got six guests right now, not counting the one on the table. Like I said, it's quiet. And even during our busiest times, most of our storage space goes unused. It's rare for us to be half full. We just like to be prepared for the worst."

"Any fresh bodies in stock?" Mr. Crepsley asked.

"Wait a minute and I'll check," Jimmy said. He consulted a large pad and flicked through a few pages. "There's a man in his thirties," Jimmy said. "Died in a car crash just over eight hours ago."

"Nothing fresher?" Mr. Crepsley asked.

"Afraid not," Jimmy replied.

Mr. Crepsley sighed. "It will have to do."

"Wait a minute," I said. "You're not going to drink from a dead person, are you?"

"No," Mr. Crepsley said. He reached inside his cape and pulled out some of the small bottles where he stored his supply of human blood. "I have come for a refill."

"You can't!" I yelled.

"Why not?" he asked.

"It isn't right. It's not fair to drink from the dead. Besides, the blood will have turned sour."

"It will not be at its best," Mr. Crepsley agreed, "but it will do for bottling. And I disagree: A corpse is the ideal person to drain, since it has no use for the blood. It will take a lot to fill these bottles. Too much to take from a living person."

"Not if you took a little from several," I protested.

"True," he said. "But that would require time, effort, and risk. It is easier this way."

"Darren doesn't speak like a vampire," Jimmy remarked.

"He is still learning." Mr. Crepsley grunted. "Now, lead the way to the body, please. We have not got all night."

I knew it would be pointless to argue anymore, so I shut my mouth and followed silently behind them.

Jimmy slid out the body of a tall blond man and whipped back the sheet. There was a nasty bruise on the dead man's head and his body was really white, but otherwise he looked like he might be sleeping.

Mr. Crepsley made a long, deep cut across the man's chest, baring his heart. He arranged the bottles beside the corpse, then got out a tube and stuck one end into the first of the bottles. He stuck the other end into the dead man's heart, then wrapped his fist around the organ and squeezed it like a pump.

Blood crept slowly along the tube and into the bottle. When it was almost full, Mr. Crepsley pulled the tube out and jammed a cork into the neck of the bottle. He stuck the mouth of the tube into the second bottle and started filling that one.

Raising the first bottle, he swallowed a mouthful and rolled it around his gums, as though tasting wine. "Good," he grunted, licking his lips. "It is pure. We can use it."

He filled eight bottles, then turned to me with a serious look on his face.

"Darren," he said, "I know you are reluctant to drink human blood, but it is time you got over your fear."

"No," I said immediately.

"Come now, Darren," he growled. "This person is dead. His blood is no good to him anymore."

"I can't," I said. "Not from a corpse."

"But you will not drink from a live person!" Mr. Crepsley exploded. "You will have to drink human blood eventually. This is the best way to start."

"Um, listen, guys," Jimmy said. "If you're going to feed, I think I should get out of —"

"Quiet!" Mr. Crepsley snapped. His eyes were

burning into me. "You have to drink," he said firmly. "You are a vampire's assistant. It is time you behaved like one."

"Not tonight," I begged. "Another time. When we go hunting. From a living person. I can't drink from a corpse. It's disgusting."

Mr. Crepsley sighed and shook his head. "One night you will realize how silly you are being," he said. "I just hope, by that time, you are not beyond being saved."

Mr. Crepsley thanked Jimmy Ovo for his help, and the two started talking about the past and their friends. I sat by myself while they chatted, feeling miserable, wondering how long I could go without human blood.

When they were finished, we walked downstairs. Jimmy came with us and waved good-bye. He was a nice guy and I was sorry we'd had to meet under dark circumstances.

Mr. Crepsley didn't say anything the whole way home, and when we arrived back at the Cirque Du Freak, he tossed me angrily to one side and pointed a finger at me.

"If you die," he said, "it is not my fault."

"Okay," I replied.

"Stupid boy," he grumbled, then stormed off to his coffin.

I stayed up a while longer and watched the sun rising. I thought a lot about my situation and what would happen when my strength faded and I began to die. A half-vampire who wouldn't drink blood; it would have been funny if it wasn't so deadly.

What should I do? That was the question that kept me awake long after the sun rose. What should I do? Forget about it and just drink human blood? Or stay true to my humanity and . . . *die?*

CHAPTER TWENTY

I STAYED INSIDE MY TENT most of the day and didn't even go out to say hi to Sam when he came around. I was so sad. I didn't feel like I belonged anywhere anymore. I couldn't be a human and wouldn't be a vampire. I was somewhere in between the two.

I got a lot of sleep that night, and the next day I felt better. The sun was shining, and although I knew my problems hadn't gone away, I was able to overlook them for a while.

Evra's snake was sick. She'd picked up a virus, and Evra had to stay in to look after her.

When Sam showed up, we decided to visit that old deserted railroad station of his. Evra didn't mind being left behind. He'd come with us another time.

The railroad station was cool. There was a huge circular yard paved with cracked stones, a three-story house that had served as the guard's house, a couple of old sheds, and several abandoned train cars. There were also railroad tracks running everywhere you looked, overgrown with weeds and grass.

Sam and I walked along some of the tracks and pretended we were on tightropes way above the ground. Every time one of us slipped, he had to scream and pretend to fall fatally to earth. I was much better at the game than Sam, because my vampire powers meant my sense of balance was better than any human's.

We explored a few of the old cars. A couple were run down, but most were okay. Pretty dusty and dirty, but otherwise in good condition. I couldn't understand why they'd been left there to rot.

We climbed onto the roof of one of the cars and stretched out to sit in the sun.

"You know what we should do?" Sam said after a while.

"What?" I asked.

"Become blood brothers."

I propped myself up on an elbow and stared. "Blood brothers?" I asked. "What for? And how's it done?"

"It'd be fun," he said. "We each make a small cut

on one of our hands, then join them together and swear an oath to be best friends forever."

"That sounds all right," I agreed. "Do you have a knife?"

"We can use some glass," Sam said. He slid over to the edge of the roof, reached down, and snapped a piece of glass out of one of the train-car windows. When he came back, he made a small cut in the fleshy part of his palm, then handed me the glass.

I was about to cut my palm when I remembered the vampire blood in my veins. I didn't think a small amount could do Sam any harm, but then again . . .

I lowered the glass and shook my head.

"No," I said. "I don't want to do it."

"Come on," Sam urged. "Don't be afraid. You only have to make a small cut."

"No," I said again.

"Coward!" he yelled. "You're afraid! Chicken! Coward!" He began to sing: "Fraidy cat, fraidy cat!"

"Okay, I'm a coward." I laughed. It was easier to lie than tell the truth. "Everybody's afraid of something. I didn't see you rushing to wash the wolf-man the other day."

Sam made a face. "That's different."

"Horses for courses," I said smugly.

"What does that mean?" he asked.

"I'm not sure," I admitted. "It's something my dad used to say."

We joked around some more, then hopped down and crossed the yard to the guard's house. The doors had rotted off years ago, and most of the glass in the windows had fallen out. We walked through a couple of small rooms, then into a larger one, which had been the living room.

There was a huge hole in the middle of the floor, which we carefully avoided.

"Look up," Sam told me.

I did and discovered I was gazing directly at the roof. The floors in between had fallen in over the years, and all that was left of them were jagged edges around the sides. I could see sunlight shining through a couple of holes in the roof.

"Follow me," Sam said, and he led me to a staircase at the side of the room. He started up. I followed slowly, not sure if it was the smartest thing to do — the steps were creaky and looked as though they might collapse — but not wanting to be called a chicken twice in the same day.

We stopped at the third floor, where the stairs stopped. You could touch the roof from there, and we did.

"Can we get out on the roof?" I asked.

"Yes," Sam said, "but it's too dangerous. The shingles are loose. You could slide off. Anyway, there's something better up here than the roof."

He walked along the side of the uppermost room of the house. The ledge was about two feet wide most of the way, but I kept my back to the wall, not wanting to take any chances.

"This section of floor won't collapse, will it?" I asked nervously.

"It never has before," Sam replied. "But there's a first time for everything."

"Thanks for putting my mind at ease," I grumbled.

Sam stopped a little farther on. I craned my neck so I could see past him and realized we had come to a set of rafters. There were six or seven of them, long pieces of wood stretching from one side of the room to the other.

"This used to be the attic," Sam explained.

"I guessed that," I told him.

He looked back at me and grinned. "But can you guess what we're going to do next?" he asked.

I stared at him, then down at the rafters. "You don't mean . . . You aren't going to . . . You're going to walk across, right?"

"Right," he said, and set his left foot on the rafter.

"Sam, this isn't a good idea," I said. "You looked unsteady on the railroad tracks. If you stumble up here . . ."

"I won't," he said. "I was only fooling down there."

He set his other foot on the wooden rafter and began walking. He went slowly, his arms stretched out on either side. My heart was in my throat. I was certain he'd fall. I looked down and knew he wouldn't survive if he fell. There were four stories if you included the basement. It was a long drop. A deadly one.

But Sam made it across safely to the other side, where he turned and took a bow.

"You're crazy!" I yelled.

"No," he said, "just brave. How about *you?* Dare to chance it? It'd be easier for you than it was for me."

"What do you mean?" I asked.

"Chickens have wings!" he shouted.

That did it! I'd show him!

Taking a deep breath, I went across, moving quicker than Sam had, making full use of my vampire abilities. I didn't look down and tried not to think about what I was doing and in a couple of seconds I was across and standing beside Sam.

"Wow!" He was impressed. "I didn't think you'd do it. Certainly not so quickly."

"You don't travel with the Cirque without picking up a few tricks," I said, pleased with myself.

"Do you think *I* could go that fast?" Sam asked.

"I wouldn't try it," I advised him.

"I bet you can't do it again," he dared me.

"Just watch," I said, and darted back across, even faster.

We spent a fun few minutes crossing over and back, taking each of the rafters in turn. Then we crossed at the same time, on different rafters, yelling and laughing at each other.

Sam stopped in the middle of his rafter and turned to face me.

"Hey!" he shouted. "Let's play mirrors."

"What's that?" I asked.

"I do something and you have to copy me." He shook his left hand above his head. "Like this."

"Oh," I said, and shook my hand. "Okay. As long as you don't jump to your death. That's the one thing I *won't* copy."

He laughed, then made a face. I made one, too. Then he slowly stood on one leg. I did the same. Next he bent and touched his toes. I followed his example. I couldn't wait until it was my turn. I'd do a few things — like jump from one rafter to the next — that there was no way he could copy. For once, I was glad for my vampire blood.

Of course, that was the moment when it went and let me down

There was no warning. One second I was beginning to stand, having bent to touch my toes. The next my head was spinning, my arms were flapping, and my legs were shaking.

This wasn't my first dizzy spell — I'd had several recently — but I hadn't taken much notice before — I'd just sat down and waited for the dizziness to pass. This time was different. I was four stories up. There was nowhere to sit.

I tried lowering myself, thinking I could cling to the rafter and crawl to safety. But before I could get low enough, my feet slipped out from under me . . . and I fell!

CHAPTER TWENTY-ONE

ALTHOUGH MY VAMPIRE BLOOD was responsible for getting me into the mess on the rafters, it also saved my life.

As I fell, I stuck out an arm — more out of desperation than anything else — and my hand caught the rafter. If I'd been an ordinary human boy, I wouldn't have had the strength to hold on. But I wasn't ordinary. I was a half-vampire. And even though I was dizzy, I was able to grab tight and hold on.

I swung above the four-story drop, eyes shut, hanging on by those four slim fingers and my thumb.

"Darren! Hang on!" Sam shouted. He didn't need to tell me that — I was hardly going to let go.

I'm coming over," Sam said. "I'll be there as fast as I can. Don't let go. And don't panic."

He went on talking as he made his way across, calming me down, telling me it would be all right, he'd rescue me, I had to relax, everything was fine.

His words helped. They gave me something other than the drop to think about. If not for Sam, I would have been a goner.

I felt him inch out along my rafter. The wood creaked, and for one awful moment I thought the weight would cause it to break and send both of us plummeting to our deaths. But it held and he closed the gap, crawling along on his stomach, quickly but carefully.

Sam paused when he reached me.

"Now," he said, "I'm going to grab your wrist with my right hand. I'll do it slowly. Don't move while I'm doing it, and don't grab me with your free hand. Okay?"

"Okay," I said.

I felt his hand close over my wrist.

"Don't let go of the rafter," he said.

"I won't," I promised.

"I don't have the strength to pull you up," he told me, "so I'm going to swing you from one side to the other. Stretch your free arm out. When you can, grab for the rafter. If you miss, don't panic, I'll still be holding on. If you get a grip, stay still for a few seconds and give your body a chance to relax. Then we can haul you up. Got it?"

"Got it, captain," I said, grinning nervously.

"Here goes. And remember: Everything will be all right. Okay. It's going to work. You will survive."

He began swinging me, lightly at first, then a little harder. I was tempted to grab at the rafter after a few swings but forced myself to wait. When I thought I was swinging high enough, I stretched out my fingers, concentrated on the thin plank of wood, and grabbed.

I caught it!

I was able to relax a little then and rest the muscles of my right arm.

"Do you feel ready to pull yourself up?" Sam asked.

"Yes," I said.

"I'll help you get your upper body up," he said. "When your stomach is safe across the rafter, I'll get out of the way and give you room to bring your legs up."

Sam put his right hand on the collar of my shirt and jacket — to catch me if I slipped — and helped yank me upward.

I scraped my chest and stomach on the rafter, but the pain didn't bother me. In fact, I welcomed it: It meant I was alive.

When I was safe, Sam backed off and I got my legs up. I crawled after him, moving slower than necessary. When I reached the ledge, I stayed crouched down and didn't stand until we got to the stairs. Then I leaned against the wall and let out a long, shuddering sigh of relief.

"Wow," Sam said to the left of me. "That was *fun!* Do you want to do it again?"

I *think* he was joking.

CHAPTER TWENTY-TWO

LATER, AFTER I'D STUMBLED down the stairs — my sense of balance was still off, but getting better — we walked back to the train cars and rested in the shadow of one.

"You saved my life," I said softly.

"It was nothing," Sam said. "You would have done the same for me."

"Probably," I said. "But I wasn't called upon to help. I wasn't the one who had to use his head and act cool. You saved me, Sam. I owe you my life."

"Keep it." He laughed. "What would *I* do with it?"

"I'm serious, Sam. I owe you big-time. Anything you ever want or need, just ask, and I'll do anything to get it for you."

"You mean that?"

"Cross my heart," I swore.

"There is *one* thing," he said.

"Name it."

"I want to join the Cirque Du Freak."

"Saaaammmm . . . ," I groaned.

"You asked what I wanted, so I'm telling you," he replied.

"It's not that easy," I protested.

"Yes it is," he said. "You can talk to the owner and put in a good word for me. Come on, Darren, did you mean what you said or not?"

"All right." I sighed. "I'll ask Mr. Tall."

"When?"

"Today," I promised. "As soon as I get back."

"All right!" Sam tried to high-five me.

"But if he says no," I warned him, "that's the end of it, okay? I'll do what I can, but if Mr. Tall says no, that *means* no."

"Sure," Sam said. "That's fine by me."

"Maybe there's a job for me, too," somebody said behind my back.

I spun around quickly, and there was R.V., smiling strangely.

"You shouldn't creep up on people like that," I snapped. "You scared me."

"Sorry, man," R.V. said, but he didn't look very sorry.

"What are you doing out here?" Sam asked.

"I wanted to find Darren," R.V. said. "I never got a chance to thank him for my ticket."

"That's okay," I said. "I'm sorry I wasn't around to see you when it was over, but I had to go somewhere else."

"Sure," R.V. said, sitting down on the track beside me. "I can understand that. A show that size, there must be lots to do, huh? I bet they keep you real busy, right, man?"

"Right," I said.

R.V. grinned, and stared at the two of us. There was something about the way he was smiling that made me uneasy. It wasn't a nice smile.

"Tell me," R.V. said, "how's the wolf-man doing?"

"He's fine," I said.

"He's chained up all the time, isn't he?" R.V. asked.

"No," I said, remembering Evra's warning.

"He's not?" R.V. acted surprised. "A wild beast like him, savage and dangerous, and he isn't locked up?"

"He's not really dangerous," I said. "That's an act. He's pretty tame, actually." I could see Sam staring at me. He knew how wild the wolf-man was and didn't get why I was lying.

"Tell me, man, what does a thing like that eat?" R.V. asked.

"Steak. Pork chops. Sausages." I forced a smile. "The usual stuff. All store-bought."

"Really? What about the goat that spider bit? Who eats that?"

"I don't know."

"Evra said the two of you bought the goat from a local farmer. Did it cost much?"

"Not really," I said. "It was pretty sick, so it —"

I stopped. Evra had told R.V. we bought the goat from a *butcher*, not a farmer.

"I've been doing a little investigating, man," R.V. said softly. "Everybody else in my camp has been getting ready to move on, but I've been walking around, counting sheep and cows, asking questions, digging for bones.

"Animals have been vanishing," R.V. continued. "The farmers aren't taking much notice — they don't mind the odd one or two missing — but it intrigues me. Who do you think could be taking them, man?"

I didn't answer.

"Another thing," he said. "I was walking along the river you're camped by, and do you know what I found downstream? Lots of small bones and scraps of skin and meat. Where do you think they could have come from, Darren?"

"I don't know," I said. Then I stood up. "I gotta go now. They need me back at the Cirque. Jobs to do."

"Don't let me keep you," R.V. said with a smile.

"When is your group headed out?" I asked. "I might stop by to say good-bye before you leave."

"That's nice of you," R.V. said. "But don't worry, man. I won't be going anywhere soon."

I frowned. "I thought you said you were moving on."

"NOP is moving on," he said. "In fact, they've already moved. They pulled out yesterday evening." He smiled icily. "But *I'm* staying a little longer. There are a few things I want to check out."

"Oh." Inside my head I swore loudly, but outside I pretended to be happy. "That's good news. Well, see you around."

"Oh, yeah," R.V. said. "You'll see me around, man. You can bet on that. You'll be seeing *plenty* of me."

I grinned awkwardly.

"So long for now," I said.

"So long," R.V. replied.

"Wait up," Sam called. "I'll come with you."

"No," I said. "Come tomorrow. I'll have an answer from Mr. Tall for you by then. Bye."

I took off before either of them could say anything else.

R.V.'s interest in the disappearance of the animals worried me at first, but as I walked back to camp I began to relax. When all was said and done, he was only a hairy harmless human, while those of us in the Cirque Du Freak were strange, powerful beings. What could he possibly do to hurt us?

CHAPTER TWENTY-THREE

I MEANT TO REPORT right to Mr. Tall when I got back, to tell him about R.V., but as I was heading for his van, Truska — the lady who was able to grow an incredible beard — grabbed my arm and made signs that she wanted me to follow her.

She led me to her tent. It was decorated more than most of the other tents and vans. The walls were covered with mirrors and paintings. There were huge wardrobes and dressing tables and a humongous four-poster bed.

Truska said something in her weird seal-like voice, then stood me in the center of the room and made a sign that I wasn't supposed to move. She grabbed a measuring tape and measured my body.

When she finished, she pursed her lips and thought for a few seconds, then clicked her fingers and hurried to one of the closets. She dug through it, coming out with a pair of pants. She found a shirt in another closet, a jacket in another, and a pair of shoes in a large chest. She let me pick my own T-shirt, under-wear, and socks from one of the dressing-table drawers.

I stepped behind a silk screen to put the clothes on. Evra must have told her about my wish to find new clothes. I'm glad that he did, because I probably would have kept on forgetting.

Truska clapped her hands when I came out and quickly shoved me in front of a mirror. The clothes fit perfectly and, much to my surprise, I looked super-cool! The shirt was light green, the pants were dark purple, and the jacket was blue and gold. Truska found a long piece of red satin cloth and wrapped it around my waist like a belt. That completed the pic-ture: I looked just like a pirate!

"This is great!" I told her. "The only thing is," I said, pointing at my feet, "the shoes are a little tight."

Truska took back the shoes and found a new pair. They were roomier than the first pair and the toes curled up just like Sinbad the Sailor's. They were really cool.

"Thanks, Truska," I said, and started to leave. She raised a hand and I stopped. She pulled a chair over to one of the taller wardrobes and stood on it, reached up, and brought down a huge round box. She plopped it on the floor, opened it, and pulled out a small brown hat with a feather in it, the kind that Robin Hood wore.

Before I could put the hat on, she made me sit down, got a pair of scissors, and gave me a haircut, which I badly needed.

The haircut and hat were the icing on the cake. I almost didn't recognize myself in the mirror when I looked this time.

"Oh, Truska," I said. "I . . . I . . ." I couldn't find the words, so instead I threw my arms around her and gave her a big, sloppy kiss. I felt embarrassed when I let go, and was glad none of my friends had been around to see, but Truska was beaming.

I rushed off to show Evra my new look. He thought the clothes were great, but swore he'd never asked Truska to help me. He said she must have either been sick of seeing me look so scruffy, or Mr. Crepsley had asked her to fix me up, or she'd done it because she liked me.

"She does not like me!" I shouted.

"Truska loves Darren," he sang. "Truska loves Darren."

"Oh, shut up, you slimy excuse for a reptile," I growled.

He laughed, not the least bit offended.

"Darren and Truska sitting in a tree," he sang, "k-i-s-s-i-n-g. First comes love, then comes marriage, then comes Darren with the vampire carriage."

I jumped on him, wrestled him to the ground, and wouldn't let go until he cried for mercy.

When we were finished. Evra went back to taking care of his snake, and I went outside and continued with the day's jobs. I was on the go nonstop, because I had to cover for Evra and do the work of two. With all that coming and going, and the excitement of having new clothes, I totally forgot about R.V. and telling Mr. Tall about the ecowarrior's threat to investigate the disappearing animals.

If I hadn't been so forgetful, maybe things would have turned out differently, and maybe our stay wouldn't have ended in a bloodbath.

CHAPTER TWENTY-FOUR

I WAS READY TO COLLAPSE by the time night came. The activity had worn me out. Evra had warned me not to sleep in his tent that night; his snake was in a foul mood because of the virus and might bite. So I headed for Mr. Crepsley's van and made a bed on the floor beside Madam Octa's cage.

I fell asleep within a couple of minutes of lying down.

A little later, as I was dreaming, something caught in my throat and made me gag. I coughed and awoke.

There was a figure above me, holding a small bottle to my mouth, trying to force a liquid down me. My first strange, terrified thought was: "It's Mr. Tiny!"

I bit the top off the bottle, cutting my lips and spilling most of the liquid. The man swore, grabbed my chin, and pried my gums apart. He tried pouring the last of the liquid into my open mouth, but I spat it out.

The man swore again, then let go and slumped back. As my heartbeat slowed, I saw that it wasn't Mr. Tiny.

It was Mr. Crepsley.

"What the hell were you trying to do?" I screamed angrily. I was too mad to feel the pain in my cut lips.

He showed me the remains of the small bottle . . . one of the containers he used to store human blood.

"You were trying to get me to drink!" I screamed.

"You have to," Mr. Crepsley said. "You are wasting away, Darren. If you go on like this, you will be dead within a week. If you do not have the courage to drink, it must be forced into you."

I stared at him savagely. He looked uncomfortable and turned his eyes away from mine.

"I was trying to help," he said.

"If you ever try that again," I said slowly, "I'll kill you. I'll wait until day, then creep in and chop your head off."

He could tell I was serious, because he nodded glumly.

"Never again," he agreed. "I knew it would not work, but I had to try. If you had swallowed even a little, it would have kept you going a while longer, and once you had the taste, you might not be so afraid to drink again."

"I'll never have the taste!" I roared. "I won't drink human blood. I don't care if I *do* die. I won't drink it."

"Very well." He sighed. "I have done my best. If you insist on being stupid, on your own head be it."

"I'm not being stupid. . . . I'm being *human*," I growled.

"But you are not human," he said softly.

"I know," I replied. "But I want to be. I want to be like Sam. I want a family and ordinary friends. I want to grow old at the usual rate. I don't want to spend my life drinking blood and feeding off humans, worrying about sunlight and vampire hunters."

"Too bad," Mr. Crepsley said. "It is the hand you have been dealt."

"I hate you," I snarled.

"Too bad," he said again. "You are stuck with me. If it is any compensation," he added, "I am none too fond of you, either. Turning you into a half-vampire was the worst mistake I ever made."

"So why not free me?" I wailed.

"I cannot," he said. "I would if I could. Of course, you are free to leave any time you like."

I stared at him suspiciously. "Really?" I asked.

"Really," he said. "I do not mind. In fact, I would prefer it if you did. That way, you would no longer be my responsibility. I would not have to watch you die."

I shook my head slowly. "I don't understand you at all," I said.

He smiled, almost tenderly. "Nor I you," he said.

We laughed a little then, and things returned to normal. I didn't like what Mr. Crepsley had tried, but understood why he'd tried it. You can't really hate someone who has your best interests at heart.

I told him what I'd done that day, about going to the railroad yard with Sam and how he saved my life. I also told him about almost becoming Sam's blood brother.

"It is a good thing you stopped when you did," Mr. Crepsley said.

"What would have happened if I hadn't?" I asked.

"Your blood would have tainted his. He would have developed a taste for raw meat. He would have hung around butcher shops, staring in the windows. He would have aged at a slightly slower rate than normal. It would not have been much of a difference, but it would have been enough."

"Enough to do what?" I asked.

"Drive him mad," Mr. Crepsley said. "He would not have understood what was happening. He would have thought he was evil. He would not have known why his life had changed. Within ten years he would have been a screaming wreck."

I shivered at the thought of how close I'd come to destroying Sam's life. This sort of thing was precisely why I had to stay with Mr. Crepsley until I'd learned everything about being a half-vampire.

"What do you think of Sam?" I asked.

"I have not seen much of him," Mr. Crepsley said. "He comes mostly by day. But he seems nice. Very bright."

"He's been helping Evra and me with our chores," I said.

"I know."

"He's a good worker."

"So I have heard."

I licked my lips nervously. "He wants to join the Cirque," I said. Mr. Crepsley's face darkened. "I was going to ask Mr. Tall, but I forgot. I'll ask tomorrow. What do you think he'll say?"

"He will say you have to ask *me*. Children cannot join the Cirque Du Freak unless an independent member agrees to be their guardian.

"*I* could be his guardian," I said.

"You are not old enough. It would have to be me. I would have to give my permission. But I will not."

"Why?" I asked.

"Because it is a crazy idea," he said. "One child is bad enough. There is no way I would take on a second. Besides, he is human. I am stuck with you because of the vampire blood in your veins. Why should I put my neck on the line for a human?"

"He's my friend," I said. "He'd be company for me."

Mr. Crepsley snorted. "Madam Octa is company enough."

"That's not the same," I whined.

"Tell me this," Mr. Crepsley mused. "What happens when he finds out you are a vampire? You think he will understand? You think he will sleep easily, knowing his best friend would like nothing better than to slit his throat open and drink him dry?"

"I wouldn't do that!" I yelled.

"I know," Mr. Crepsley agreed. "But I am a vampire. I know what you are really like. So do Mr. Tall, Evra, and the others. But how do you think an ordinary human would see you?"

I sighed unhappily. "You won't let him join?"

Mr. Crepsley began to shake his head, then stopped and nodded slowly. "Very well," he said. "He can join."

"He *can?*" I stared at him, shocked. Even though I'd been arguing on Sam's behalf, I'd never really thought they would let him join.

"Yes," Mr. Crepsley said. "He can join and travel with us and help you and Evra with your jobs. But on one condition." Mr. Crepsley leaned in close to me and grinned wickedly. *"He has to become a half-vampire, too!"* he hissed.

CHAPTER TWENTY-FIVE

My heart was heavy when I saw Sam run into camp early the next morning. I hated having to disappoint him but knew I had to. There was no way I could let Mr. Crepsley turn Sam into a half-vampire.

I'd thought about it a lot during the night, and the frightening thing was, I believed Sam would agree to become a half-vampire if I gave him the option. Smart as he was, I don't think he'd have stopped to consider the loneliness and awfulness of being a vampire.

He rushed over when he saw me, too excited to notice my new clothes and haircut.

"Did you ask him? Did you?" His face was bright, filled with hope.

"Yes," I said, smiling sadly.

"And?"

I shook my head. "Sorry, Sam. He said no."

Sam's face fell about a thousand miles.

"*Why?*" he shouted.

"You're too young," I said.

"You're not much older!" he snapped.

"But I don't have parents," I lied. "I didn't have a home when I joined the Cirque."

"I don't care about my parents," he said with a sniff.

"That's not true," I said. "You'd miss them."

"I could go home for holidays."

"It wouldn't work. You're not cut out for life in the Cirque Du Freak. Maybe later, when you're older."

"I don't care about *later!*" he yelled. "I want to join *now*. I've worked hard. I've proved myself. I kept quiet when you were lying to R.V. about the wolf-man yesterday. Did you tell that to Mr. Tall?"

"I told him everything," I said.

"I don't believe you," Sam said. "I don't think you spoke to him at all. I want to see him myself."

I shrugged and pointed toward Mr. Tall's van. "That's where you'll find him," I said.

Sam ran off in a huff but slowed after a few steps, then came to a halt. He kicked the ground miserably, then returned and sat down beside me.

"It's not fair," he grumbled. I could see tears trickling down his cheeks. "I made up my mind to join. It was going to be great. I had it all planned."

"There'll be other chances," I said.

"When?" he asked. "I've never heard of a freak show playing around here before. When will I run into one again?"

I didn't answer.

"You wouldn't have liked it, anyway," I said. "It's not as much fun as you think. Imagine what it's like in the middle of winter, when you have to get up at five in the morning and shower in ice-cold water and work outside in blizzards."

"That doesn't bother me," Sam insisted. Then his tears stopped and he got a crafty look in his eyes. "Maybe I'll come along, anyway," he said. "Maybe I'll sneak into one of the vans and stow away with you. Mr. Tall would have to take me then."

"You can't do that!" I snapped. "No way!"

"I will if I want." He grinned. "You can't stop me."

"Yes, I can," I growled.

"How?" He sneered.

I took a deep breath. The time had come to scare Sam Grest away forever. I couldn't tell him the truth about me, but I could invent a story almost as horrifying, one guaranteed to send him running.

"I never told you what happened to my parents,

did I, Sam? Or how I came to join the freak show?" I kept my voice low and steady.

"No," Sam said quietly. "I've wondered a lot, but I didn't want to ask."

"I killed them, Sam," I said.

"*What?*" His face went white.

"I go crazy sometimes. Like the wolf-man. Nobody knows when it's going to happen, or why. I was in a hospital when I was younger, but I seemed to be getting better. My parents brought me home for Christmas. After dinner, while I was in a fight with Dad, I flipped out.

"I tore him to pieces. Mom tried to drag me off, but I killed her too. My little sister ran for help, but I caught her. I ripped her apart the same way I'd ripped my mother and father.

"Then, after I'd killed them . . ." I locked eyes with Sam. It had to be a good act to make him believe. "*I ate them.*"

He stared at me, stunned.

"That's not true," he whispered. "It can't be."

"I killed and ate them, then ran away," I lied. "I was discovered by Mr. Tall, who agreed to hide me. They have a special cage built to keep me in when I go crazy. The problem is, nobody knows when it's going to happen. That's why most people avoid me. Evra's okay, because he's strong. So are some of the other performers. But ordinary humans . . . I could rip them apart in a second."

"You're lying," Sam said.

I picked up a large stick lying nearby, turned it around in my hands, then put it in my mouth and bit through it like it was a big carrot.

"I'd chew your bones and spit you out as gristle," I told Sam. I'd cut my lips on the stick and the blood made me look ferocious. "You wouldn't be able to stop me. You'd be sleeping in my tent if you joined the show and would be the one I'd go for first.

"You can't join the Cirque Du Freak," I said. "I wish you could — I'd love to have a friend — but it's not possible. I'd end up killing you if you joined."

Sam tried responding but couldn't get his mouth to work. He believed my big lie. He'd seen enough of the show to know that things like that *could* happen here.

"Go away, Sam," I said sadly. "Go away and don't ever come back. It's safer that way. It's better. For both of us."

"Darren, I . . . I . . ." He shook his head uncertainly.

"*Go!*" I roared, and pounded the ground with my hands. I bared my teeth and growled. I was able to make my voice much deeper than a human's, so it sounded like a wild animal.

Sam screamed, scrambled to his feet, and sprinted for the woods, never once looking back.

I watched him go, heavyhearted, certain my ploy had worked. He'd never be back. I wouldn't see him again. Our paths had separated, and we would never meet again.

If I'd known how wrong I was — if I'd had any idea of the awful night that lay ahead — I'd have run after him and never returned to that disgusting circus of blood, that revolting circus of *death*.

CHAPTER TWENTY-SIX

I WAS MOPING AROUND when one of the Little People tapped me on the back. It was the one with the limp.

"What do you want?" I asked.

The tiny man — if it was a man — in the blue-hooded robe rubbed his stomach with his hands. This was the sign that he and his brothers were hungry.

"You just had breakfast," I said.

He rubbed his stomach again.

"It's too early for lunch."

He rubbed his stomach again.

I knew that this would go on for hours if I let it. He would patiently follow me around, rubbing his stomach, until I agreed to go hunt for food for him.

"All right," I snapped. "I'll see what I can find. But I'm on my own today, so if I don't come back with a full bag, tough."

He rubbed his stomach again.

I spit on the ground and took off.

I shouldn't have gone hunting. I was really weak. I could still run faster than a human, and I was stronger than most kids my age, but I wasn't superfit or extrastrong anymore. Mr. Crepsley had said I'd be dead within a week if I didn't drink human blood, and I knew he'd spoken the truth. I could feel myself wasting away. A few more days and I wouldn't be able to pull myself out of bed.

I tried catching a rabbit but wasn't fast enough. I worked up a sweat chasing it and had to sit down for a few minutes. Next, I went looking for roadkill but couldn't find any dead animals. Finally, because I was tired and half afraid of what would happen if I returned to camp empty-handed (the Little People might decide to eat *me!*), I headed for a field full of sheep.

They were grazing peacefully when I arrived. They were used to humans and barely lifted their heads when I entered the field and walked among them.

I was looking for an old sheep, or one that looked sick. That way I wouldn't have to feel so lousy about killing it. I finally found one with skinny, trembling legs and a dazed expression, and decided she'd do. She looked as though she didn't have long to live, anyway.

If I'd had my full powers, I would have snapped

her neck and she would have been dead in an instant, without any pain. But I was weak and clumsy and didn't twist hard enough the first time.

The sheep began to bleat with agony.

She tried running away, but her legs wouldn't carry her. She fell to the ground, where she lay bleating miserably.

I tried breaking her neck again but couldn't. In the end I grabbed a stone and finished the job. It was a messy, horrible way to kill an animal, and I felt ashamed of myself as I grabbed its back legs and hauled it away from the flock.

I'd almost reached the fence before I realized somebody was sitting on top of it, waiting for me. I dropped the sheep and looked up, expecting an angry farmer.

But it wasn't a farmer.

It was R.V.

And he was mad as hell.

"How could you?" he shouted. "How could you kill a poor, innocent animal so cruelly?"

"I tried killing her quickly," I said. "I tried snapping her neck, but I couldn't. I was going to leave her when I couldn't do it, but she was in pain. I thought it was better to finish her off than leave her to suffer."

"That's real big of you, man," he said sarcastically.

"Do you think you'll get the Nobel Peace Prize for that?"

"Come on, R.V.," I said. "Don't be angry. She was sick. The farmer would have killed her anyway. Even if she'd lived she would have been sent to a butcher in the end."

"That don't make it right," he said angrily. "Just because other people are nasty, it don't mean you should be nasty, too."

"Killing animals isn't nasty," I said. "Not when it's for food."

"What's wrong with vegetables?" he asked. "We don't need to eat meat, man. We don't need to kill."

"*Some* people need meat," I disagreed. "Some can't live without it."

"Then they should be left to die!" R.V. roared. "That sheep never did any harm to anyone. As far as I'm concerned, killing her is worse than killing a human. You're a murderer, Darren Shan."

I shook my head sadly. There was no point arguing with somebody this stubborn.

"Look, R.V.," I said. "I don't enjoy killing. I'd be psyched if every person in the world was a vegetarian. But they're not. People eat meat, and that's a fact of life. I'm only doing what I have to."

CHAPTER TWENTY-SIX

"Well, we'll see what the police have to say about it," R.V. said.

"The police?" I frowned. "What do they have to do with it?"

"You've killed somebody else's sheep." He laughed cruelly. "Do you think they'll let you get away with that? They won't arrest you for murdering rabbits and foxes, but they'll charge you for killing a sheep. I'll have the police and health inspectors come down on you like a ton of bricks." He grinned.

"You won't!" I gasped. "You don't like the police. You're always fighting against them."

"When I have to," he agreed. "But when I can get them on my side . . ." He laughed again. "They'll arrest you first, then turn your camp upside down. I've been studying the goings-on there. I've seen the way you treat that poor hairy man."

"The wolf-man?"

"Yeah. You keep him locked away like an animal."

"He *is* an animal," I said.

"No," R.V. disagreed. "*You* are the animal, man."

"R.V., listen," I said. "We don't have to be enemies. Come back to camp with me. Talk to Mr. Tall and the others. See how we live. Get to know and understand us. There's no need to —"

"Save it," he snapped. I'm getting the police. Nothing you can say will stop me."

I took a deep breath. I liked R.V. but knew I couldn't allow him to destroy the Cirque Du Freak.

"All right, then," I said. "If nothing I *say* can stop you, maybe you'll respond to something I *do*."

Summoning all my remaining strength, I threw the dead body of the sheep at R.V. It struck him in the chest and knocked him flying from the fence. He yelled with surprise, then with pain as he landed heavily on the ground.

I leaped over the fence and was on him before he could move.

"How did you do that, man?" he whispered.

"Never mind," I snapped.

"Kids can't throw sheep," he said. "How did —"

"Shut up!" I shouted, and slapped his bearded face. He stared up at me, shocked. "Listen, Reggie Veggie," I growled, using the name he hated, "and listen good. You *won't* go to the police or the health inspectors. Because if you do, the sheep won't be the only dead body I drag back to the Cirque Du Freak today."

"What are you?" he asked. His voice was trembling, and his eyes were filled with terror.

"I'm the end of you if you screw with me," I swore.

I dug my fingernails into the soil at either side of his face and squeezed his head between my hands, just enough to let him know how strong I was.

"Get out of here, Reggie," I said. "Go find your friends in NOP. Stick to protesting against new roads and bridges. You're in over your head here. Me and my friends in the Cirque are freaks, and freaks don't obey the same laws as other people. Understand?"

"You're crazy," he whimpered.

"Yes," I said. "But not as crazy as you'll be if you stay and interfere."

I stood and draped the sheep over my shoulders.

"Going to the police would be useless, anyway," I said. "By the time they reach the camp, this sheep will be long gone, bones and all.

"You can do what you like, R.V. Stay or go. Report me to the police or keep your mouth shut. It's up to you. All I have left to say is this: To me and my kind, you're no different from this sheep." I gave it a shake. "We'd think no more of killing you than we would any dumb animal in the fields."

"You're a monster!" R.V. yelled.

"Yeah," I agreed. "But I'm only a *baby* monster. You should see what some of the others are like." I smiled nastily at him, hating myself for acting so mean, but knowing this was the way it had to be. "So long, Reggie Veggie," I said sarcastically, and walked away.

I didn't look back. I didn't need to. I could hear the chattering of his terrified teeth practically all the way back to camp.

CHAPTER TWENTY-SEVEN

THIS TIME I WENT straight to Mr. Tall and told him about R.V. He listened carefully, then said, "You handled him well."

"I did what I had to," I replied. "I'm not proud of it. I don't like bullying or scaring people, but there was no other way."

"Actually, you should have killed him," Mr. Tall said. "That way he could do us no harm whatsoever."

"I'm not a murderer," I told him.

"I know." He sighed. "Nor am I. It's a pity one of the Little People wasn't with you. They'd have chopped his head off without a second's hesitation."

"What do you think we should do?" I asked.

"I don't think he can cause many problems," Mr. Tall said. "He'll probably be too scared to go to the police right away. Even if he does, there's no evidence against you. It would be an unwanted complication, but we've had plenty of dealings with officers of the law in the past. We could cope.

"The health authorities worry me more. We could hit the road and lose them, but people in the health department tend to trail you around like hound dogs once they've got your scent.

"We'll leave tomorrow," he decided. "There's a show scheduled for tonight, and I hate canceling on short notice. Dawn is the earliest any health inspector could be here, so we'll make sure we're gone before then."

"You're not angry with me?" I asked.

"No," he said. "This isn't the first time we've clashed with the public. You're not to blame."

I helped Mr. Tall spread the word of our departure. Everybody took it in stride. Most seemed happy to be getting this much notice; a lot of times they had to move on with only an hour or two of warning.

It was another busy day for me. As well as preparing for the show, I had to help people get ready for leaving. I offered to help Truska pack her stuff, but her tent was already bare when I got there. She only winked when I asked how she'd packed so quickly.

When Mr. Crepsley awoke I told him about our plan to leave. He didn't seem surprised.

"We have been here long enough," he said.

I asked to be left out of that night's show, because I wasn't feeling very well.

"I'll get to bed early," I said, "and get a good night's sleep."

"It will not do any good," Mr. Crepsley warned. "There is only one thing that will make you feel better, and you know what it is."

Night rolled on, and soon it was time for the show to begin. There was another big crowd. The roads were blocked with cars in both directions. Everybody in the Cirque was busy, either preparing to go onstage or getting people seated or selling stuff.

The only two who seemed to have nothing to do were me and Evra, who wasn't performing because of his sick snake. He left her for a few minutes to watch the start of the show. We stood on one side of the stage as Mr. Tall got the ball rolling and introduced the wolf-man.

We stuck around until the first break, then walked outside and studied the stars.

"I'll miss this place when we go," Evra said. "I like the country. You can't see stars as well in the city."

"I didn't know you were interested in astronomy," I said.

"I'm not," he replied. "But I like looking up at the stars."

I got dizzy after a while and had to sit down.

"You're not feeling too good, are you?" Evra asked.

I smiled weakly. "I've been better."

"Still not drinking human blood?" I shook my head. He sat beside me. "You've never told me *exactly* why you won't drink it," he said. "It can't be so different from animal blood, can it?"

"I don't know," I said. "And I don't want to find out." I paused. "I'm afraid that if I drink human blood, I'll be *evil*. Mr. Crepsley says vampires aren't evil, but I think they are. I think anyone who looks at humans as if they're animals *must* be evil."

"But if it keeps you alive . . . ," Evra said.

"That's how it would start," I said. "I'd tell myself I was doing it to keep going. I'd swear never to drink more than I needed. But what if I couldn't stop myself? I'll need more as I grow older. What if I couldn't control my thirst? What if I killed someone?"

"I don't think you could," Evra said. "You're *not* evil, Darren. I don't think a good person can do evil things. As long as you treat human blood like medicine, you'll be all right."

"Maybe," I said, although I didn't believe it. "Anyway, I'm okay for now. I don't have to make a final decision for a couple more days."

CHAPTER TWENTY-SEVEN

"Would you really let yourself die rather than drink?" Evra asked.

"I don't know," I answered honestly.

"I'd miss you if you died," Evra said sadly.

"Well," I said uncomfortably, "maybe it won't come to that. Maybe there's some other way I can survive, a way that Mr. Crepsley doesn't want to tell me about until he has no other choice."

Evra grunted. He knew as well as I did that there was no other way.

"I'm going to check on my snake," he said. "Do you want to come and sit with us for a while?"

"No," I said. "I'd better get some sleep. We have to get up early, and I'm really tired."

We said good night. I didn't head straight for Mr. Crepsley's van but wandered through the campsite, thinking about my conversation with Evra, wondering what it would feel like to die. I'd "died" once before, and been buried, but that wasn't the same thing. If I died for real, I'd be dead for good. Life would be over, my body would decay, and then . . .

I glanced up at the stars. Was *that* where I'd be heading? To the other side of the universe? Vampire Paradise?

It was a weird time. When I was living at home I'd hardly ever thought about death; it was something that only happened to old people. Now here I was, almost face to face with it.

If only somebody else could decide for me. I should be worrying about school and making the soccer team, not about whether I should drink human blood or let myself die. It wasn't fair. I was too young. I shouldn't have to —

I saw a shadow passing the front of a nearby tent but didn't pay much attention. It wasn't until I heard a sharp snapping sound that I wondered who it might be. Nobody should have been out there. Everyone involved with the show was in the big tent. Was it somebody from the audience?

I decided to investigate.

I headed in the direction that the shadow had taken. It was a dark night, and after a few turns I couldn't figure out which way the person had gone. I was on the verge of abandoning the search when I heard another sharp snapping sound, closer this time.

I looked around and knew immediately where the sounds must have come from: *the wolf-man's cage!*

Taking a deep breath to steady my nerves, I ran as fast as I could to check it out.

CHAPTER TWENTY-EIGHT

THE GRASS WAS DAMP, so it bent beneath my feet and made no sound. When I reached the last van before the wolf-man's cage, I stopped and listened.

There was a soft jangling sound, as though heavy chains were being lightly shaken.

I stepped out from under cover.

There were dim lights on either side of the wolf-man's cage, so I was able to see everything in perfect detail. He'd been wheeled back here after his act, like he was every night. There was a slab of meat in his cage, which normally he'd be feasting on. But not tonight. Tonight he was focused on something different.

There was a big man in front of the wolf-man's cage. He had a huge pair of pliers with him and had cut some of the chains that were holding the door shut.

The man was trying to unwrap the chains but wasn't doing very well. He swore softly to himself and lifted the pliers to cut through another link.

"What are you doing?" I shouted.

The man jumped with shock, dropped the pliers, and spun around.

It was, as I had guessed, R.V.

He looked guilty and scared at first, but when he saw I was alone he grew in confidence.

"Stay back!" he warned.

"What are you doing?" I demanded.

"Freeing this poor, abused creature," he said. "I wouldn't keep the wildest of animals in a cage like this. It's inhumane. I'm letting him go. I called the police — they'll be out here in the morning — but I decided to do a little work of my own beforehand."

"You can't do that!" I shrieked. "Are you crazy? That guy's savage. He'd kill everything within a five-mile radius if you let him out!"

"So *you* say," R.V. sneered. "I don't believe that. It's been my experience that animals react according to how they're treated. If you treat them like crazy monsters, they'll act that way. If, on the other hand, you treat them with respect, love, and humanity . . ."

"You don't know what you're doing," I told him.

"The wolf-man isn't like other animals. Walk away from there before you do any real damage. We can talk it over. We can —"

"No!" he screamed. "I'm through talking!"

He spun back to the chains and began struggling with them again. He reached into the cage and tugged the thickest chains through the bars. The wolf-man watched him silently.

"R.V., stop!" I shouted, and raced over to stop him from opening the door. I grabbed his shoulders and tried pulling him away, but I wasn't strong enough. I punched him in the ribs a few times, but he only grunted and doubled his efforts.

I grabbed for his hands, to pry them off the chains, but the bars were in the way.

"Leave me alone!" R.V. yelled. He turned his head to speak to me directly. His eyes were wild. "You won't stop me!" he screamed. "You won't prevent me from doing my duty. I'll free this victim. I'll see justice done. I'll —"

He stopped ranting all of a sudden. His face turned deathly white and his body shuddered, then went stiff.

There was a crunching, munching, ripping sound, and when I looked inside the cage, I realized the wolf-man had made his move.

He'd sprung across the cage while we were arguing, grabbed both of R.V.'s arms, jammed them in his mouth, and *bitten them off below the elbows!*

R.V. fell away from the cage, shocked. He lifted his shortened arms and watched as blood pumped from the holes at the ends of his elbows.

I tried grabbing his lower arms back from the mouth of the wolf-man — if I could retrieve them, they could be stuck back on — but he moved too quickly for me, leaped back out of reach, and began chewing. Within seconds the arms were a mess, and I knew they'd never be any good again.

"Where are my hands?" R.V. cried.

I switched my attention back to him. He was staring at the stumps that were his arms, a funny look on his face, not yet feeling the pain.

"Where are my hands?" he cried again. "They're gone. They were there a minute ago. Where did all this blood come from? Why can I see the bone inside my skin?

"Where are my hands?" He screamed this last question at the top of his lungs.

"You have to come with me," I said frantically. "We have to take care of your arms before you bleed to death."

"Stay away from me!" R.V. yelled. He tried raising a hand to shove me back, then remembered he didn't have hands anymore.

"You're responsible for this!" he shouted. "You did this to me!"

"No, R.V., it was the wolf-man," I said, but he wasn't listening.

"This is your fault," he insisted. "You took my hands. You're an evil little monster, and you stole my hands. My hands! My hands!"

He began screaming again. I reached for him, but this time he brushed me aside, turned, and ran. He tore screaming through the camp, his blood-drenched half-arms raised high above his head, yelling as loudly as he could, until he vanished into the night.

"My hands! My hands! My hands!"

I wanted to run after him but was afraid he might attack me. I ran off to find Mr. Crepsley and Mr. Tall — they'd know what to do — but was stopped dead in my tracks by a worrying growl behind me.

I turned slowly. The wolf-man was at the door of the cage, which was swinging wide open! He'd somehow removed the last of the chains and freed himself.

I remained perfectly still as he stood and grinned viciously, his long, sharp teeth glinting in the dim light.

He looked to the left and to the right, stretched out his hands, and grabbed the bars on either side. Then he crouched down low and tensed his legs.

He sprang, propelling himself toward me.

I shut my eyes and waited for the end to come.

I heard and felt him land about a foot in front of me. I began to say my final prayers.

But then I heard him flying overhead and realized he'd bounced over me. For a couple of terrifying seconds I waited for his teeth to bite through the back of my neck and gnaw my head off.

But they didn't.

Confused, I turned, blinking. He was racing away from me! I saw a figure ahead of him, running quickly between the trailers, and realized he was after somebody else. He'd passed me up for a tastier meal!

I took several stumbling steps after the wolf-man. I was smiling and silently thanking the gods. I couldn't believe how close I'd just come to death. When he'd leaped through the air, I was sure —

My feet struck something, and I stopped.

I looked down and saw a bag. The person the wolf-man was chasing must have dropped it, and for the first time I wondered who it was that the wild wolf-man was after.

I picked up the bag. It was the kind you carry over

one shoulder. It was full of clothes, which I could feel through the cover. A small jar fell out as I turned the bag around. Retrieving it, I opened the lid and caught the bitter smell of . . . pickled onions!

My heart almost stopped. I began searching furiously for a name tag, praying the pickled onions didn't mean what I feared.

My prayers went unanswered.

The handwriting, when I found it, was neat but unjoined. The writing of a child.

"This bag is the property of Sam Grest," it said, and his address was just beneath. "Hands off!!" it warned at the end, which was pretty ironic given what had happened a minute or so earlier to R.V.

But I didn't have time to laugh at my twisted, dark joke.

Sam! For some reason he snuck out here tonight — probably to stow away with the Cirque — and must have seen and followed me. It was Sam the wolf-man's beady eyes had spotted, standing behind me. It was Sam running for his life through the camp.

The wolf-man was after Sam!

CHAPTER TWENTY-NINE

I SHOULDN'T HAVE CHASED them on my own. I should have gone for help. It was crazy, rushing off into the darkness by myself.

But he was after Sam. Sam, who wanted to join the Cirque. Sam, who asked to be my blood brother. Harmless, friendly, long-winded Sam. The boy who'd saved my life.

I didn't think about my own safety. Sam was in trouble, and there wasn't time to seek anyone else's help. It might be the death of me, but I had to go after them, to try to save Sam. I owed him.

I got out of the camp quickly. The clouds had parted overhead and I spotted the wolf-man disappearing into the trees. I hurried after him, running as fast as I could.

I heard the wolf-man howl a while later, which was a good sign. It meant he was still chasing Sam. If he'd caught him, he'd be too busy eating to howl.

I wondered why he hadn't caught him yet. He should have. Although I'd never seen him running in the open, I was sure he must be fast. Maybe he was playing with Sam, toying with him before he moved in for the kill.

Their footprints were clear in the damp night earth, but I would have been able to follow from their sounds anyway. It's hard to run silently through a forest, especially at night.

We ran in that way for a few minutes, Sam and the wolf-man way in front and out of sight, me trailing behind. My legs were beginning to get really tired, but I forced myself on.

I thought about what I'd do when I caught up. There was no way I could beat the wolf-man in a fair fight. I could smash him over the head with a stick or something, but probably not. He was strong and fast, and had the taste for human blood. He'd be pretty much unstoppable.

The most I could hope to do was throw myself in his path and take Sam's place. If I offered myself instead of Sam, maybe he'd take me and Sam could escape.

I wouldn't mind dying for Sam. I'd given up my humanity for one friend; it wasn't asking so much more to give up my life for another.

Besides, this way, if I died, it would be for a good cause. I wouldn't have to worry anymore about drinking human blood or starving to death. I could go down fighting.

After a few more minutes, I ran into a clearing and realized where Sam had led us: the old deserted railroad station.

It showed he was still thinking clearly. This was the best place to come, with plenty of hiding spots and lots of stuff — chunks of metal and glass — to use in a fight. Maybe neither of us would have to die. Maybe there was a chance we could win this battle.

I saw the wolf-man pause in the middle of the station yard and sniff the air. He howled again, a loud spine-shivering howl, then sprinted toward one of the rusty train cars.

I ran around the back of the car, moving as quietly as I could. I listened for sounds when I got there but couldn't hear anything. I lifted myself up and looked in one of the windows: nothing.

I lowered myself and slid along to the third window over. I couldn't see anything when I looked inside again.

I was lifting myself to peek in the next window, when I suddenly saw a metal bar moving toward my face at high speed.

I twisted to my side just in time to avoid it. It whistled by my face, scratching me but not doing any serious damage.

"Sam, stop, it's *me!*" I hissed, dropping to the ground. There was silence for a moment, then Sam's face appeared in the round window.

"Darren?" he whispered. "What are you doing here?"

"I followed you," I said.

"I thought you were the wolf-man. I was trying to kill you."

"You practically did."

"I'm sorry."

"For God's sake, Sam, don't waste time apologizing," I snapped. "We're in big trouble. We've got to think. Get out here quick."

He backed away from the window. There were soft shuffling sounds, then he appeared outside the car door. He looked to make sure the wolf-man wasn't around, jumped down, and crept over to me.

"Where is he?" Sam asked.

"I don't know," I whispered. "He's around somewhere, though. I saw him coming in this direction."

"Maybe he found something else to attack." Sam whispered back hopefully. "A sheep or a cow."

"I wouldn't bet on it," I said. "He wouldn't have run all this way just to abandon the chase at the very end."

We huddled close together, Sam covering the right with his eyes, me the left. I could feel his body trembling, and I'm sure he could feel mine shaking, too.

"What are we going to do?" Sam asked.

"I don't know," I whispered. "Any ideas?"

"A couple," he said. "We could lead him into the guard's house. He might fall through the rotten floorboards. We could trap him down there."

"Maybe," I said. "But what if *we* fall through, too? We'd be trapped. He could jump down and eat us whenever he liked."

"How about the rafters?" Sam asked. "We could climb out into the middle of a rafter and hang on, back to back. We could take sticks with us and beat him off if he attacked. There'd only be one way for him to come at us up there."

"And somebody's got to arrive from the Cirque Du Freak sooner or later," I whispered, thinking it over. "But what if he decides to snap the rafter at one end?"

"They're set pretty deeply into brick," Sam said. "I don't think he could break them with his bare hands."

"Would a rafter hold the weight of three of us?" I asked.

"I'm not sure," Sam admitted. "But at least if we fell from that height it'd be over quickly. Who knows, we might get lucky and fall on the wolf-man. He could break our fall and get killed in the process."

I laughed weakly. "You watch too many cartoons. But that's a good idea. Better than any I can think of."

"How long do you think it'll be before the people from the Cirque get here?" Sam whispered.

"Depends on when they realize what's happening," I said. "If we're lucky, they'll have heard him howling and might be here in a couple of minutes. Otherwise we might have to wait until the end of the show, which could be another hour, maybe longer."

"Do you have a weapon?" Sam asked.

"No," I said. "I didn't have time to pick anything up."

He handed me a short iron bar. "Here," he said. "I had this for backup. It's not very good, but it's better than nothing."

"Any sign of the wolf-man?" I asked.

"No," he said. "Not yet."

"We'd better get going before he arrives," I whispered, then stopped. "How are we going to get to the guard's house? It's a far hike, and the wolf-man could be hiding anywhere along the way."

"We'll have to run for it and hope for the best," Sam said.

"Should we split up?" I asked.

"No," he said. "I think we're better off together."

"Okay. Are you ready to start?"

"Gimme a few seconds," he said.

I turned and watched him breathing. His face was white, and his clothes were ripped and dirty from running through the woods, but he looked ready to fight. He was a tough little character.

"Why did you come back tonight, Sam?" I whispered.

"To join the Cirque Du Freak," he answered.

"Even after everything I told you about me?"

"I decided to risk it," he said. "I mean, you're my friend. We have to stick by our friends, right? Your story made me want to join more, once I'd recovered from being scared. Maybe I could have helped you. I've read books about personality disorders. Maybe I could have cured you."

I couldn't help smiling in the middle of this horrifying moment we were in. "You're a moron, Sam Grest," I whispered.

"I know." He smiled. "So are you. That's why we make a good team."

"If we get out of this," I told him, "feel free to join. And you don't have to worry about me eating you. That was just a story to frighten you off."

"Really?" he asked.

"Really," I said.

"Phew." He wiped his brow. "I can rest easy now."

"You can if the wolf-man doesn't get you," I said with a grin.

"Ready yet?"

"I'm ready." He squeezed his palms and prepared to run. "On the count of three," he whispered.

"Okay," I replied.

"One," he began.

We faced in the direction of the guard's house.

"Two."

We got in position to sprint.

"Thr—"

Before he could finish, a pair of hairy hands darted out from underneath the car, where — I realized too late — the wolf-man was hiding. The fingers wrapped around Sam's lower legs, grabbed him by the ankles, and dragged him down to the ground.

CHAPTER THIRTY

SAM STARTED TO SCREAM as soon as the hands tightened on his ankles. The fall knocked the breath out of him, silencing him momentarily, but after a second or two he was screaming again.

I scrambled to my knees, grabbed Sam's arms, and pulled as hard as I could.

I could see the wolf-man underneath the car, spread out on his hairy belly and grinning wildly. Drool was dripping from his jaws.

I pulled with all my might, and Sam slid toward me. But the wolf-man came with him, wriggling out from under the car, not loosening his grip.

I stopped pulling and let go of Sam. I grabbed the iron bar that he'd dropped, jumped to my feet, and began pounding the outstretched arms of the wolf-man, who howled angrily.

The wolf-man released one of his hairy paws and swatted at me. I ducked out of the way and struck at the hand still holding Sam. The wolf-man yelped with pain and his fingers came free.

"Run!" I screamed to Sam as I yanked him to his feet.

We sprinted toward the guard's house, side by side. I could hear the wolf-man scrambling out from beneath the car. He'd been playing with us before, but now he was furious. I knew he'd come at us with everything he had. The games were over. There was no way we'd make it to the guard's house. He'd have us before we were halfway across the yard.

"Keep . . . running," I gasped to Sam, then stopped momentarily and looked back to meet the charge of the oncoming wolf-man.

My actions took him by surprise, and he ran into me. His body was hairy and sweaty and heavy. The collision sent both of us flying to the ground. Our arms and legs were all tangled up, but I quickly freed myself and whacked him with the iron bar.

The wolf-man roared angrily and swiped at my arm. This time he connected, just below where it joined with my shoulder. The force of the blow deadened my arm, which became a useless lump of flesh and bone. I dropped the bar, then reached for it with my other hand.

But the wolf-man was quicker. He snatched up the bar and tossed it far away, where it fell with a clang, lost to the darkness.

He stood slowly, grinning nastily. I could read the expression in his eyes and knew, if he could speak, he would be saying something like: "Now, Darren Shan, you're mine! You had your fun and games, but now it's killing time!"

He grabbed my body by the sides, opened his mouth wide, and leaned forward to bite my face off. I could smell the stench of his breath and see bits of meat and shirt from R.V.'s arms stuck between his yellow teeth.

Before he could snap his jaws shut, something hit the side of his head and knocked him off-balance.

I could see Sam behind him, a heavy chunk of wood in his hands. He hit the wolf-man again, this time making his hands let go.

"One good turn deserves another!" Sam screamed crazily, slamming the wood into the wolf-man for a third time. "Come on! We have to —"

I never heard Sam's next words. Because as I started toward him, the wolf-man lashed out blindly with one of his fists. It was a wild shot, but he got lucky and it slammed into my face, knocking me backward.

My head almost exploded. I saw bright lights and huge stars, then slumped to the ground, passed out.

When I came to a few seconds or minutes later — I don't even know how much time had passed — the railroad station was eerily quiet. I couldn't hear anybody running or screaming or fighting. All I could hear was a steady munching sound, a little way ahead of me.

Munch, munch, munch.

I sat up slowly, ignoring the hammering pain in my head.

It took my eyes a few seconds to readjust to the darkness. When I could see again, I realized I was gazing at the back of the wolf-man. He was crouched on all fours, head bent over something. *He* was the one making the munching sounds.

The dizziness from the punch meant it took me a while to realize it wasn't a some*thing* he was eating . . . it was a some*one*.

SAM!!!

I scrambled to my feet, pain forgotten, and rushed forward, but one look at the bloody mess beneath the wolf-man and I knew I was too late.

"*NO!*" I screamed and punched the wolf-man with my one good hand, attacking senselessly.

He grunted and shoved me away. I sprang back and this time kicked as well as punched. He growled and tried shoving again, but I held on and pulled his hair and ears.

He howled then and finally lifted his mouth. It was red, a dark, awful red, full of guts and blood and pieces of flesh and bone.

He rolled on top of me, forcing me down, and pinned me with one long, hairy arm. His head shot back and he howled up at the night sky. Then, with a demonic snarl, he drove his teeth toward my throat, meaning to finish me off with one quick bite.

CHAPTER THIRTY-ONE

AT THE LAST POSSIBLE MOMENT, a pair of hands appeared out of the darkness and grabbed the wolf-man's jaw, stopping his plunge.

The hands twisted the head to one side, causing the wolf-man to shriek and fall off me.

His attacker climbed onto his back and held him down. I saw fists flying faster than my eyes could follow, and then the wolf-man was lying unconscious on the ground.

His attacker stood and pulled me to my feet. I found myself gazing up into the flushed, scarred face of Mr. Crepsley.

"I came as soon as I could," the vampire said somberly, turning my head gently to the left and right, examining the damage. "Evra heard the howls of the wolf-man. He did not know about you and the boy. He just thought the creature had burst free.

"Evra told Mr. Tall, who canceled the rest of the show and organized a search party. Then I thought of *you*. When I saw your bed was empty, I searched around and found your trail."

"I thought . . . I was going to . . . die," I moaned, finding it hard to speak. I was bruised all over and suffering from shock. "I was certain. I thought . . . nobody would come. I . . ."

I threw my good arm around Mr. Crepsley and hugged him hard.

"Thank you," I sobbed. "Thank you. Thank you. Thank —"

I stopped, remembering my fallen friend.

"Sam!" I screamed. I let go of Mr. Crepsley and rushed to where he was lying.

The wolf-man had torn Sam's stomach open and eaten a lot of his insides. Amazingly, Sam was still alive when I got to him. His eyelids were fluttering, and he was breathing lightly.

"Sam, are you okay?" I whispered. It was a stupid question, but the only one my trembling lips could form. "Sam?" I brushed his forehead with my fingers, but he showed no signs of hearing or feeling me. He just lay there, with his eyes staring up at me.

Mr. Crepsley knelt down beside me and checked Sam's body.

"Can you save him?" I cried. He shook his head slowly. "You have to!" I shouted. "You can close the wounds. We can call a doctor. You can give him a potion. There must be some way to —"

"Darren," he said softly, "there is nothing we can do. He is dying. The damage is too great. Another couple of minutes and . . ." He sighed. "At least he is beyond feeling. There will be no pain."

"No!" I screamed, and threw myself onto Sam. I was crying bitterly, sobbing so hard it hurt.

"Sam! You can't die! Sam! Stay alive! You can join the Cirque and travel with us all over the world. You can . . . you . . ."

I could say no more, only lower my head, cling to Sam, and let the tears pour down my face.

In the deserted old railroad yard, the wolf-man lay unconscious behind me. Mr. Crepsley sat silently by my side. Underneath me, Sam Grest — who'd been my friend and saved my life — lay perfectly still and slipped further and further into the final sleep of an unfair and horrible death.

CHAPTER THIRTY-TWO

AFTER A WHILE, I felt somebody tugging at the sleeve of my left arm. I looked around. Mr. Crepsley was standing over me, looking miserable.

"Darren," he said, "it will not seem like the right time, but there is something you must do. For Sam's sake. And your own."

"What are you talking about?" I wiped some of the tears from my face and stared up at him. "Can we save him? Tell me if we can. I'll do anything."

"There is nothing we can do to save his *body*," Mr. Crepsley told me. "He is dying and nothing can change that. But there is something we can do for his *spirit*.

"Darren," he said, *"you must drink Sam's blood."*

I went on staring at him, but now it was a stare of disbelief, not hope.

"How could you?" I whispered with disgust. "One of my best friends is dying, and all you can think about . . . You're sick! You're a sick, twisted monster. You should be dying, not Sam. I hate you. Get out of here."

"You do not understand," he said.

"Yes I do!" I screamed. "Sam's dying, but all you're worried about is blooding me. Do you know what you are? You're a no-good —"

"Do you remember our discussion about vampires being able to absorb part of a person's spirit?" he asked.

I was just about to call him something awful, but his question confused me.

"What's that got to do with this?" I asked.

"Darren, this is important. Do you remember?"

"Yes," I said softly. "What about it?"

"Sam is dying," Mr. Crepsley said. "A few more minutes and he will be gone. Forever. But you can keep part of him alive within you if you drink from him now and take his life before the wounds of the wolf-man can."

I couldn't believe what I was hearing.

"You want *me* to kill Sam?" I screamed.

"No," he sighed. "Sam has already been killed. But if you finish him off before he dies from the bites of the wolf-man, you will save some of his memories and feelings. In you he can live on."

I shook my head. "I can't drink his blood," I whispered. "Not Sam's." I glanced down at the small, savaged body. "I can't."

Mr. Crepsley sighed. "I will not force you to," he said. "But think carefully about it. What happened tonight is a tragedy that will haunt you for a very long time, but if you drink from Sam and absorb part of his essence, dealing with his death will be easier. Losing a loved one is hard. This way, you need not lose all of him."

"I can't drink from him," I sobbed. "He was my friend."

"It is *because* he was your friend that you must," Mr. Crepsley said, then turned away and left me to decide.

I stared down at Sam. He looked so lifeless, like he'd already lost everything that made him human, alive, unique. I thought of his jokes and long words and hopes and dreams, and how awful it would be if all of that just disappeared with his death.

Kneeling, I placed the fingers of my left hand on Sam's red neck. "I'm sorry, Sam," I moaned, then dug my sharp nails into his soft flesh, leaned forward, and stuck my mouth over the holes they'd made.

Blood gushed in and made me gag. I nearly fell away, but with an effort I held my place and gulped it down. His blood was hot and salty and ran down my throat like thick, creamy butter.

Sam's pulse slowed as I drank, then stopped. But I went on drinking, swallowing every last drop, absorbing.

When I'd finally sucked him dry, I turned away and howled at the sky like the wolf-man had. For a long time that's all I could do, howl and scream and cry like the wild animal of the night that I'd become.

CHAPTER THIRTY-THREE

MR. TALL AND A BUNCH of others from the Cirque Du Freak — including four Little People — arrived a little later. I was sitting by Sam's side, too tired to howl anymore, staring blankly into space, feeling his blood settle in my stomach.

"What's the story?" Mr. Tall asked Mr. Crepsley. "How did the wolf-man get free?"

"I do not know, Hibernius," Mr. Crepsley replied. "I have not asked and do not intend to, not for a night or two at least. Darren is in no shape for an interrogation."

"Is the wolf-man dead?" Mr. Tall asked.

"No," Mr. Crepsley said. "I merely knocked him out."

"Thank heaven for small mercies." Mr. Tall sighed. He clicked his fingers and the Little People chained up the unconscious wolf-man. A van from the show pulled up and they bundled him into the back.

I thought about demanding the wolf-man's death, but what good would it have been? He wasn't evil, just naturally mad. Killing him would have been pointless and cruel.

When they'd finished with the wolf-man, the Little People's attention turned to Sam's shredded remains.

"Hold on," I said, as they bent to pick him up and cart him away. "What are they going to do with Sam?"

Mr. Tall coughed uncomfortably. "I, ah, imagine they intend to *dispose* of him," he said.

It took me a moment to realize what that meant. "They're going to *eat* him?" I shrieked.

"We can't just leave him here," Mr. Tall reasoned, "and we don't have time to bury him. This is the easiest —"

"No," I said firmly.

"Darren," Mr. Crepsley said, "we should not interfere with —"

"No!" I shouted, striding over to shove the Little People backward. "If they want to eat Sam, they'll have to eat me first!"

The Little People stared at me wordlessly, with hungry green eyes.

"I think they'd be quite happy to accommodate you," Mr. Tall said drily.

"I mean it," I growled. "I won't let them eat Sam. He deserves a proper burial."

"So that worms can devour him?" Mr. Tall asked, then sighed when I glared at him, and shook his head irritably.

"Let the boy have his way, Hibernius," Mr. Crepsley said quietly. "You may return to the Cirque with the others. I will stay and help dig the grave."

"Very well." Mr. Tall shrugged. He whistled and pointed a finger at the Little People. They hesitated, then backed away and crowded around the owner of the Cirque Du Freak, leaving me alone with the dead Sam Grest.

Mr. Tall and his assistants left. Mr. Crepsley sat down beside me.

"How are you?" he asked.

I shook my head. There was no simple answer to that.

"Do you feel stronger?"

"Yes," I said softly. Even though it hadn't been long since I'd drank Sam's blood, already I noticed a difference. My eyesight had improved and so had my hearing, and my battered body didn't hurt nearly as much as it should.

"You will not have to drink again for a long time," he said.

"I don't care. I didn't do it for me. I did it for Sam."

"Are you angry with me?" he asked.

"No," I said slowly.

"Darren," he said, "I hope —"

"I don't want to talk about it!" I snapped. "I'm cold, sore, miserable, and lonely. I want to think about Sam, not waste words on you."

"As you wish," he said, and began digging in the soil with his fingers. I dug beside him in silence for a few minutes, then paused and looked over.

"I'm a real vampire's assistant now, aren't I?" I asked.

He nodded sadly. "Yes. You are."

"Does that make you glad?"

"No," he said. "It makes me feel ashamed."

As I stared at him, confused, a figure appeared above us. It was the Little Person with the limp. "If you think you're taking Sam . . . ," I warned him, raising a dirt-encrusted hand. Before I got any further, he jumped into the shallow hole, stuck his wide, gray-skinned fingers into the soil, and clawed up large clumps.

"He's helping us?" I asked, puzzled.

"It seems like it," Mr. Crepsley said, and laid a

hand on my back. "Rest," he advised. "We can dig faster by ourselves. I will call you when it is time to bury your friend."

I nodded, crawled out, and lay down on the bank beside the quickly forming grave. After a while I shuffled out of the way and sat, waiting, in the shadows of the old railroad station. Just me and my thoughts. And Sam's dark, red blood on my lips and between my teeth.

CHAPTER THIRTY-FOUR

WE BURIED SAM WITHOUT much talk — I couldn't think of anything to say — and filled in the grave. We didn't hide it, so he'd be discovered by the police and given a real burial soon. I wanted his parents to be able to give him a ceremony, but this would keep him safe from scavenging animals (and Little People) in the meantime.

We broke camp before dawn. Mr. Tall told everybody there was a long trek ahead. Sam's disappearance would create a fuss, so we had to get as far away as possible.

I wondered, as we left, what had become of R.V. Did he bleed to death in the forest? Did he make it to a doctor in time? Or was he still running and screaming, "My hands! My hands!"?

I didn't care. Although he'd been trying to do the

right thing, this was R.V.'s fault. If he hadn't gone messing with the locks on the wolf-man's cage, Sam would be alive. I didn't hope R.V. was dead, but I didn't say a prayer for him, either. I'd leave him to fate and whatever it had in store.

Evra sat beside me at the rear of the van as the Cirque pulled out. He started to say something. Stopped. Cleared his throat. Then he put a bag on my lap. "I found that," he muttered. "Thought you might want it."

Through stinging eyes I read the name — "Sam Grest" — then burst into tears and cried bitterly over it. Evra put his arms around me and held me tight and cried along with me.

"Mr. Crepsley told me what happened," Evra mumbled eventually, recovering slightly and wiping his face clean. "He said you drank Sam's blood to keep his spirit alive."

"Apparently," I replied weakly, unconvinced.

"Look," Evra said, "I know how much you didn't want to drink human blood, but you did this for Sam. It was an act of goodness, not evil. You shouldn't feel bad for drinking from him."

"I guess," I said, then moaned at the memory and cried some more.

The day went by and the Cirque Du Freak rolled on, but thoughts of Sam couldn't be left behind. As night came, we pulled over to the side of the road for a short break. Evra went to look for food and drinks.

"Do you want anything?" he asked.

"No," I said, my face pressed against the windowpane. "I'm not hungry."

He started to leave.

I called him back. "Wait a sec."

There was a strange taste in my mouth. Sam's blood was still hot on my lips, salty and terrible, but that wasn't what had started the buds at the back of my tongue tingling. There was something I wanted that I'd never wanted before. For a few confusing seconds I didn't know what it was. Then I identified the strange craving and managed to crack the thinnest of smiles. I searched Sam's bag, but the jar must have been left behind when we left.

Looking up at Evra, I wiped tears from my eyes, licked my lips, and asked in a voice that sounded a lot like that smart-ass kid I once knew, "Do we have any pickled onions?"

TO BE CONTINUED . . .

The Saga of Darren Shan
continues with

TUNNELS OF BLOOD

Book 3
in the Cirque Du Freak series

Dare to read on....

PROLOGUE

THE SMELL OF BLOOD is sickening. Hundreds of carcasses hang from silver hooks, stiff, shiny with frosty blood. I know they're just animals — cows, pigs, sheep — but I keep thinking they're human.

I take a careful step forward. Powerful overhead lights mean it's bright as day. I have to tread carefully. Hide behind the dead animals. Move slowly. The floor's slippery with water and blood, which makes progress even trickier.

Ahead, I spot him . . . the vampire . . . Mr. Crepsley. He's moving as quietly as I am, eyes focused on the fat man a little way ahead.

The fat man. He's why I'm here in this ice-cold slaughterhouse. He's the human Mr. Crepsley intends to kill. He's the man I have to save.

The fat man pauses and checks one of the hanging

slabs of meat. His cheeks are chubby and red. He's wearing clear plastic gloves. He pats the dead animal — the squeaky noise of the hook as the carcass swings puts my teeth on edge — then begins whistling. He starts to walk again. Mr. Crepsley follows. So do I.

Evra is somewhere far behind. I left him outside. No point in both of us risking our lives.

I pick up speed, moving slowly closer. Neither knows I'm here. If everything works out as planned, they won't know, not until Mr. Crepsley makes his move. Not until I'm forced to act.

The fat man stops again. Bends to examine something. I take a quick step back, afraid he'll spot me, but then I see Mr. Crepsley closing in. Damn! No time to hide. If this is the moment he's chosen to attack, I have to get nearer.

I spring forward several feet, risking being heard. Luckily Mr. Crepsley is entirely focused on the fat man.

I'm only three or four feet behind the vampire now. I bring up the long butcher's knife that I've been holding down by my side. My eyes are glued to Mr. Crepsley. I won't act until he does — I'll give him every chance to prove my terrible suspicions wrong — but the second I see him tensing to spring . . .

I take a firmer grip on the knife. I've been practicing my swipe all day. I know the exact point I want to hit. One quick cut across Mr. Crepsley's throat and that'll be that. No more vampire. One more carcass to add to the pile.

Long seconds slip by. I don't dare look to see what the fat man is studying. Is he ever going to rise?

Then it happens. The fat man struggles to his feet. Mr. Crepsley hisses. He gets ready to lunge. I position the knife and steady my nerves. The fat man's on his feet now. He hears something. Looks up at the ceiling — wrong way, idiot! — as Mr. Crepsley leaps. As the vampire jumps, so do I, screeching loudly, slashing at him with the knife, determined to kill. . . .

CHAPTER ONE

One month earlier . . .

MY NAME'S DARREN SHAN. I'm a half-vampire.

I used to be human, until I stole a vampire's spider. After that, my life changed forever. Mr. Crepsley — the vampire — forced me to become his assistant, and I joined a circus full of weird performers called the Cirque Du Freak.

Adapting was hard. Drinking blood was harder, and for a long time I wouldn't do it. Eventually I did, to save the memories of a dying friend (vampires can store a person's memories if they drain all their blood). I didn't enjoy it — the following few weeks were horrible, and I was plagued by nightmares — but after that first blood-red drink there could be no going back. I accepted my role as a vampire's assistant and learned to make the best of it.

Over the course of the next year, Mr. Crepsley taught me how to hunt and drink without being caught; how to take just enough blood to survive; how to hide my vampire identity when mixing with others. And in time I put my human fears behind me and became a true creature of the night.

A couple of girls stood watching Cormac Limbs with serious expressions. He was stretching his arms and legs, rolling his neck around, loosening his muscles. Then, winking at the girls, he put the middle three fingers of his right hand between his teeth and bit them off.

The girls screamed and fled. Cormac chuckled and wriggled the new fingers that were growing out of his hand.

I laughed. You got used to stuff like that when you worked in the Cirque Du Freak. The traveling show was full of incredible people, freaks of nature with cool and sometimes frightening powers.

Apart from Cormac Limbs, the performers included Rhamus Twobellies, capable of eating a full-grown elephant or an army tank; Gertha Teeth, who could bite through steel; the wolf-man — half man, half wolf, who'd killed my friend Sam Grest; Truska, a beautiful and mysterious woman who could grow a beard at will; and Mr. Tall, who could move as fast as lightning and seemed to be able to read people's minds. Mr. Tall owned and managed the Cirque Du Freak.

We were performing in a small town, camped behind an old mill inside which the show was staged every night. It was a run-down junkyard, but I was used to that type of venue. We could have played the grandest theaters in the world and slept in luxurious hotel rooms — the Cirque made a ton of money — but it was safer to keep a low profile and stick to places where the police and other officials rarely wandered.

My appearance hadn't changed much since leaving home with Mr. Crepsley almost a year and a half before. Because I was a half-vampire, I aged at only a fifth the rate of humans, which meant that though eighteen months had passed, my body was only three or four months older.

Although I wasn't very different on the outside, inside I was an entirely new person. I was stronger than any boy my age, able to run faster, leap farther, and dig my extra-strong nails into brick walls. My hearing, eyesight, and sense of smell had improved vastly.

Since I wasn't a full vampire, there was lots of stuff I couldn't do yet. For example, Mr. Crepsley could run at a superquick speed, which he called flitting. He could breathe out a gas that knocked people unconscious. And he could communicate telepathically with vampires and a few others, such as Mr. Tall.

I wouldn't be able to do those things until I became a full vampire. I didn't lose any sleep over it, because being a half-vampire had its bonuses: I didn't have to drink much human blood and — better yet — I could move around during the day.

It was daytime when I was exploring a garbage dump with Evra, the snake-boy, looking for food for the Little People — weird, small creatures who wore blue hooded capes and never spoke. Nobody — except maybe Mr. Tall — knew who or what they were, where they came from, or why they traveled with the Cirque. Their master was a creepy man called Mr. Tiny (he liked to eat *children!*), but we didn't see much of him at the Cirque.

"Found a dead dog," Evra shouted, holding it above his head. "It smells a little. Do you think they'll mind?"

I sniffed the air — Evra was a long way off, but I

could smell the dog from here as well as a human could up close — and shook my head. "It'll be fine," I said. The Little People ate just about anything we brought.

I had a fox and a few rats in my bag. I felt bad about killing the rats — rats are friendly with vampires and usually come up to us like tame pets if we call them — but work is work. We all have to do things we don't like in life.

There were a bunch of Little People with the Cirque — twenty of them — and one was hunting with Evra and me. He'd been with the Cirque since soon after me and Mr. Crepsley joined. I could tell him apart from the others because he had a limp in his left leg. Evra and me had taken to calling him Lefty.

"Hey, Lefty!" I shouted. "How's it going?" The small figure in the blue hooded cape didn't answer — he never did — but he patted his stomach, which was the sign we needed more food.

"Lefty says to keep going," I told Evra.

"Figures," he sighed.

As I prowled for another rat, I spotted a small silver cross in the garbage. I picked it up and brushed off the dirt. Studying the cross, I smiled. To think I used to believe vampires were terrified of crosses! Most of that stuff in old movies and books is crap. Crosses, holy water, garlic: none of those matter to vampires. We can cross running water. We don't have to be invited into a house before entering. We cast shadows and reflections (though a full vampire can't be photographed — something to do with bouncing atoms). We can't change shape or fly.

A stake through the heart will kill a vampire. But so will a well-placed bullet, or fire, or a heavy falling object. We're harder to kill than humans, but we aren't immortal. Far from it.

I placed the cross on the ground and stood back. Focusing my will, I tried making it jump into my left hand. I stared hard for all of a minute, then clicked the fingers of my right hand.

Nothing happened.

I tried again but still couldn't do it. I'd been trying for months, with no success. Mr. Crepsley made it look simple — one click of his fingers and an object would be in his hand, even if it was several feet away — but I hadn't been able to copy him.

I was getting along pretty well with Mr. Crepsley. He wasn't such a bad guy. We weren't friends, but I'd accepted him as a teacher and no longer hated him like I did when he first turned me into a half-vampire.

I put the cross in my pocket and proceeded with the hunt. After a while I found a half-starved cat in the remains of an old microwave oven. It was after rats, too.

The cat hissed at me and the hair on its neck raised. I pretended to turn my back on it, then spun quickly, grabbed it by the neck, and twisted. It gave a strangled little cry and then went limp. I stuck it in the bag and went to see how Evra was doing.

I didn't enjoy killing animals, but hunting was part of my nature. Anyway, I had no sympathy for cats. The blood of cats is poisonous to vampires. Drinking from one wouldn't have killed me, but it would have made me sick. And cats are hunters, too. The way I saw it, the less cats there were, the more rats there'd be.

That night, back in camp, I tried moving the cross with my mind again. I'd finished my jobs for the day, and the show wouldn't be starting for another couple of hours, so I had lots of time to kill.

It was a cold late-November night. There hadn't been any snow yet, but it was threatening. I was dressed in my colorful pirate costume: a light green shirt, dark purple pants, a gold-and-blue jacket, a red satin cloth around my waist, a brown hat with a feather in it, and soft shoes with toes that curled in on themselves.

I wandered away from the vans and tents and found a secluded spot around the side of the old mill.

I stuck the cross on a piece of wood in front of me, took a deep breath, concentrated on the cross, and willed it into the palm of my outstretched hand.

No good.

I shuffled closer, so my hand was only inches away from the cross.

"I command you to move," I said, clicking my fingers. "I order you to move." Click. "Move." Click. "*Move!*"

I shouted this last word louder than I meant to and stomped my foot in anger.

"What are you doing?" a familiar voice asked behind me.

Looking up, I saw Mr. Crepsley emerging out of the shadows.

"Nothing," I said, trying to hide the cross.

"What is that?" he asked. His eyes missed nothing.

"Just a cross I found while Evra and me were hunting," I said, holding it out.

"What were you doing with it?" Mr. Crepsley asked suspiciously.

"Trying to make it move," I said, deciding it was time to ask the vampire about his magic secrets. "How do you do it?"

A smile spread across his face, causing the long scar that ran down the left side to crinkle. "So that is what has been bothering you." He chuckled. He stretched out a hand and clicked his fingers, causing me to blink. Next thing I knew, the cross was in *his* hand.

"How's it done?" I asked. "Can only full vampires do it?"

"I will demonstrate again. Watch closely this time."

Replacing the cross on the piece of wood, he stood back and clicked his fingers. Once again it disappeared and turned up in his hand. "Did you see?"

"See what?" I was confused.

"One final time," he said. "Try not to blink."

I focused on the small silver piece. I heard his fingers clicking and — keeping my eyes wide open — thought I saw the slightest blur darting between me and the cross.

When I turned to look at him, he was tossing the cross from hand to hand and smiling. "Figured me out yet?" he asked.

I frowned. "I thought I saw . . . it looked like . . ." My face lit up. "You didn't move the cross!" I yelled excitedly. "*You* moved!"

He beamed. "Not as dull as you appear," he complimented me is his usual sarcastic manner.

"Do it again," I said. This time I didn't look at the cross: I watched the vampire. I wasn't able to track his movements — he was too fast — but I caught brief glimpses of him as he darted forward, snatched up the cross, and leaped back.

"So you're not able to move things with your mind?" I asked.

"Of course not." He laughed.

"Then why the click of the fingers?"

"To distract the eye," he explained.

"Then it's a trick," I said. "It's got nothing to do with being a vampire."

He shrugged. "I could not move so fast if I were human, but yes, it is a trick. I dabbled with illusions before I became a vampire, and I still like to practice."

"Could I learn to do it?" I asked.

"Maybe," he said. "You cannot move as fast as I can, but you could get away with it if the object was close to hand. You would have to practice hard — but if you wish, I can teach you."

"I always wanted to be a magician," I said. "But . . . hold on. . . ." I remembered a couple of occasions when Mr. Crepsley had opened locks with a click of his fingers. "What about locks?" I asked.

"Those are different. You understand what static energy is?" My face was a blank. "Have you ever brushed a comb through your hair and held it up to a thin sheet of paper?"

"Yeah!" I said. "The paper sticks to it."

"That is static energy," he explained. "When a vampire flits, a very strong static charge builds up. I have learned to harness that charge. Thus I am able to force open any lock you care to mention."

I thought about that. "And the click of your fingers?" I asked.

"Old habits die hard." He smiled.

"But old vampires die easy!" a voice growled behind us, and before I knew what was happening, someone had reached around the two of us and pressed a pair of razor-sharp knives to the soft flesh of our throats!

GET YOUR FREAK ON WITH

CIRQUE DU FREAK

THE *NEW YORK TIMES* BESTSELLING SERIES
BY DARREN SHAN

A LIVING NIGHTMARE

THE VAMPIRE'S ASSISTANT

TUNNELS OF BLOOD

VAMPIRE MOUNTAIN

TRIALS OF DEATH

THE VAMPIRE PRINCE

HUNTERS OF THE DUSK

ALLIES OF THE NIGHT

KILLERS OF THE DAWN

THE LAKE OF SOULS

LORD OF THE SHADOWS

SONS OF DESTINY

COLLECT THEM ALL!

Little, Brown and Company
Hachette Book Group

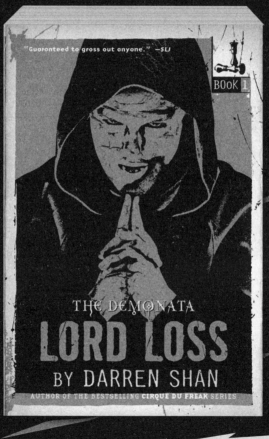